"You know anything about kids?"

Daniel questioned eagerly. "Todd's been crying for the last hour and I haven't got a clue why."

Rachel looked at Daniel. Goodness, his eyes were blue. "I had one that I managed to get through this stage without inadvertently killing him," she admitted.

"You're a godsend. Here, hold him for a minute," he said, handing the baby to Rachel.

Rachel looked down in surprise. Her arm had tingled where Daniel had touched it. That kind of electrical-impulse-upon-contact sort of thing hadn't happened to her since high school.

Suddenly the child stopped wailing and was staring fascinated at Rachel's silken tresses.

"Thank you," Daniel breathed. "You get me a couple of hours of peace and quiet and I'll be your slave forever."

Rachel laughed at that. "Yeah, right." But it was an interesting idea. A body like that, her slave?

My, oh, my.

Dear Reader,

This month Silhouette Romance has six irresistible novels for you, starting with our FABULOUS FATHERS selection, *Mad for the Dad* by Terry Essig. When a sexy single man becomes an instant dad to a toddler, the independent divorcée next door offers parenthood lessons—only to dream of marriage and motherhood all over again!

In *Having Gabriel's Baby* by Kristin Morgan, our BUNDLES OF JOY book, a fleeting night of passion with a handsome, brooding rancher leaves Joelle in the family way—and the dad-to-be insisting on a marriage of convenience for the sake of the baby....

Years ago Julie had been too young for the dashing man of her dreams. Now he's back in town, and Julie's still hoping he'll make her his bride in *New Year's Wife* by Linda Varner, part of her miniseries HOME FOR THE HOLIDAYS.

What's a man to do when he has no interest in marriage but is having trouble resisting the lovely, warm and wonderful woman in his life? Get those cold feet to the nearest wedding chapel in *Family Addition* by Rebecca Daniels.

In *About That Kiss* by Jayne Addison, Joy Mackey, sister of the bride, is sure her sis's ex-fiancé has returned to sabotage the wedding. But his intention is to walk down the aisle with Joy!

And finally, when a woman shows up on a bachelor doctor's doorstep with a baby that looks just like him, everyone in town mistakenly thinks the tiny tot is his in Christine Scott's *Groom on the Loose*.

Enjoy!

Melissa Senate, Senior Editor

Please address questions and book requests to:
Silhouette Reader Service
U.S.: 3010 Walden Ave., P.O. Box 1325, Buffalo, NY 14269
Canadian: P.O. Box 609, Fort Erie, Ont. L2A 5X3

MAD FOR
THE DAD

Terry Essig

ROMANCE™
Published by Silhouette Books
America's Publisher of Contemporary Romance

For my son Marty and all the other dedicated teachers with the Inner City Teaching Corps who struggle so hard to bring the light of reading and knowledge to Chicago's inner city.

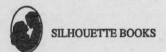 SILHOUETTE BOOKS

ISBN 0-373-19198-7

MAD FOR THE DAD

Copyright © 1997 by Terry Parent Essig

Books by Terry Essig

Silhouette Romance

House Calls #552
The Wedding March #662
Fearless Father #725
Housemates #1015
Hardheaded Woman #1044
Daddy on Board #1114
Mad for the Dad #1198

Silhouette Special Edition

Father of the Brood #796

TERRY ESSIG

says that her writing is her escape valve from a life that leaves little time for recreation or hobbies. With a husband and six children, Terry works on her stories a little at a time, between seeing to her children's piano, cello and oboe lessons, their baseball and swim team practices, and her own activities of leading a Girl Scout troop and participating in a car pool. Her ideas, she says, come from her imagination and her life—neither one of which is lacking!

Dear Todd,

When you first came to live with me, I didn't have a clue about fatherhood. And you weren't much help either, being an eighteen-month-old with a limited vocabulary. Thank God for Rachel, huh? We were a couple of sorry cases until she came along.

I'll always be grateful that when I crashed the wagon I was pulling you in, we were on Rachel's front lawn and she came out to check out our injuries. Do you realize how many variables had to fall perfectly into place for things to have worked out the way they did? Talk about fate.

So you better be on your best behavior, kid, 'cause I can't do this parenthood thing alone. I mean, Rachel thinks you're cute as a button, but that doesn't mean she wants to spend her free time with a drooling toddler and a dad-in-training who just recently recovered from Teething 101.

So remember—no crying when Rachel comes over. And maybe Uncle Daniel will get a kiss....

Love,

Daniel

Chapter One

"My, oh my, would you look at that," Rachel Gatlin commented as she propped her hip on the windowsill of her new apartment. Touching her cheek to the glass so she could get a better view down the street, she repeated, "My, oh my."

Her sister, Eileen, on the other end of the phone and across town had no such opportunity to take in the view. "I hate it when you do that," she informed Rachel. "Who's there? What are you looking at? Tell me," she commanded firmly. "It isn't anything gross, is it? We should have done a better job of checking out that neighborhood before you signed the lease. I knew it."

Gross? Not so's you'd notice, Rachel thought before responding. The scene captivating her attention was anything but disgusting. "There's this really cute guy, and I mean *really cute* guy—not that I'm swayed by externals any longer, you understand. Next time I'm going for substance—anyway, this really, *really* cute guy is coming down the block pulling a little red wagon loaded with two bags of groceries and a screaming toddler.'' She paused, studying both man and child. ''It's so much funnier when it's somebody else's screaming toddler, isn't it? And I just love it when the macho manly types have to play Mr. Mom and find out what it's all about.''

''Yeah, I do, too. Hmm, did you say really, *really* cute? Two reallies worth of cute? Let's think about this, Rachel. This could be your golden opportunity to start meeting the neighbors,'' Eileen said, and Rachel could almost hear the wheels in her brain turning through the phone line. ''Sooo,'' she continued, ''instead of sitting there admiring his body from a distance and gloating, why don't you run down there and throw yourself in front of the wagon? Introduce yourself and promise not to sue if he's willing to kiss you and make your owies all better.''

Rachel snorted inelegantly as she continued to watch the unfolding scene below. Mr. Macho had stopped the wagon in front of the two-flat next to hers. Little One had been trying to stand up. Looked like a boy from here. He was now being firmly placed back down on his little bottom. Even from two stories up, Rachel could see that the power struggle between adult and child was causing the grocery bags to list and the wagon to wobble a bit. She wanted to open the window and warn him of the impending disaster, but managed to refrain. One shouldn't interfere in a domestic squabble, she reminded herself. Too dangerous—especially a battle of the wills involving a toddler.

''Maybe next time,'' Rachel said noncommittally. ''They're already moving on, anyway.'' Besides, the guy was probably married. He was out there with a kid, wasn't he? And nobody with a backside like that—he was walking backward now in order to keep his eye on the child, so she was in a position to judge and it was good... Really good... Really, *really* good—could have survived all that long without somebody claiming him somewhere along the line. Rachel sucked in her breath. "Uh-oh. I've got to go, Eileen. Handsome just tripped over a big wheel he didn't see. He's flat on the ground right underneath my living room window." She felt an odd sense of gladness that she was being forced to act. Rachel didn't care to examine the feeling too carefully. It was simply an opportunity to meet a neighbor while performing a corporal work of mercy, that was all. It had nothing to do with his fantastic butt nor those exceptionally fine shoulders that were almost as wide as the strip of sidewalk he currently covered. She was immune to that kind of thing now.

She was sure she was.

"How can you not see a Big Wheel? What is he, blind?" Eileen asked.

"He was walking backward in order to keep his eye on the kid, all right?" Rachel said, defending the unknown man. "And right now he's on his rear end. The wagon's tipped over and there are apples and cans of something or another rolling down the sidewalk. From here, the kid looks like he's screaming his cute little head off, although he, at least, got dumped into the grass and not on the cement sidewalk. I gotta go and make sure they're all right."

"While you're out there, see if you can't find out if he's married—casually, of course," Eileen immediately urged. "You never know. He might be just baby-sitting or something."

"Yeah, right." Men that looked like Greek gods did not baby-sit in order to make ends meet, at least not in

Rachel's experience. Rachel squinted and studied him more thoroughly. No, this was no male nanny. A man with a body like that could make a fortune modeling undershorts—the snug, close-fitting kind. He was up on his hands and knees now, clearly not in need of mouth-to-mouth resuscitation. Rachel sighed in disappointment. "Even if he was free, I'm sure he'd be too young for me. I'm telling you, Eileen, I think I might have had a hot flash the other day. At the very least, it was a definite sensation of warmth."

"Oh, for heaven's sake, you're not that old. Get a grip and stop with the self-pity. Pinch your cheeks on your way down the stairs so you've got a little color and get out in front so you can see how badly they're hurt. If it's anything serious, they'll be half dead by the time you get your buns moving. Be sure to look at his ring finger when you check for broken bones. And find out where he lives. One never knows."

Rachel rolled her eyes, but rather than get involved in another discussion, she bit her tongue and kept her mouth shut.

"Call me back. I'll want all the gory details."

"In your dreams. Goodbye, Eileen."

"I mean it. Now hurry up, before somebody else beats you to him. Go."

"I'm gone. Bye." Rachel hung up the phone in defeat. Eileen was only two years older than Rachel, but Rachel had never come out on top of an argument yet. She shrugged philosophically—in the long run, she'd be proven right this time. Handsome was married and the screaming meemie down there was his, she just knew it. She grabbed the keys to her apartment from the end table over by the sofa. Then she took off out the door to check on Handsome and his little progeny, but it was only because she was a Good Samaritan and her First Aid Certificate had another six months before it expired, that was all.

By the time Rachel bounded down the steps and out the entrance of the two-flat, the object of her concern had picked himself up and was trying to comfort the toddler he now held to his chest. Little One was still exercising his vocal cords at top volume. Handsome alternated between awkwardly patting him on the back with his free hand and covering his ear—the one closest to the tyke's mouth. With his feet, he was attempting to corral cans and apples into a smaller area near the overturned wagon.

"Hi," Rachel said, breathless from doing the stairs and not from the realization that up close, the man truly was drop-dead gorgeous—not that her interest sprang from anything other than the purely aesthetic appreciation such an outstanding example of male perfection of form deserved, of course. "I saw your mishap from my window. What can I do to help?"

The man looked at her, frustration evident in his body language and written all over his face—but even so he was still as gorgeous as they came. Hair encompassing at least five different shades of color ranging all the way from white blond to brown fought to ignore the strictures of his last haircut and enjoy the light breeze. Shoulders as wide as the red wagon was long greeted Rachel at her eye level. Eyes the color of a pale blue sky hypnotized her so that she barely noticed when the man actually blushed.

"I didn't realize anyone had seen me," he said, his words barely audible over the child's carryings-on.

"Oh. Well, I just happened to be looking out the window. I'm sure nobody else did," Rachel reassured him. "My name's Rachel. I just moved in here." She waved at the gray stucco two-flat behind her. "I could use a break from unpacking boxes. Why don't you let me give you a hand for a minute or two until you've got everything back under control?"

Even though she was long past the diaper stage in her own life and she'd have little in common with the father of a toddler, the four walls of her apartment upstairs were already starting to get to her. So, she'd help him out for a bit and start meeting some of the neighbors. It was a good plan. And maybe, just maybe his wife would rent him to her for the next event she and her ex-husband, Ron, had to attend as Mark's parents. Wouldn't Ron's mouth just drop to the floor if she showed up with this hunk of masculinity at her side? The thought of there having been even a remote possibility of performing mouth-to-mouth resuscitation on this specimen practically had her mouth watering. She swallowed hard and made a stab at conversation. "Where do you live?" she asked as she averted her eyes and surveyed the wreckage.

"What? Oh, down on the corner." He gestured vaguely down the block in the direction he'd had the wagon headed before he'd crashed it.

"Well, that's not so bad then," Rachel declared optimistically. "It's what? Three houses? We can handle that. What's Little One's name?

"Todd."

"Uh-huh, and yours?"

He grimaced. "Sorry, I'm not myself at the moment. My name is Daniel. Daniel Van Scott. I'm very pleased to meet you, Rachel."

Daniel Van Scott was a gentleman, Rachel decided. With dirt smudges on his chin, grit embedded in his hands and Todd still screeching his sweet little head off two inches away from his ears, poor Daniel would be justified in being less than pleased with anything life had to offer right then, but there he stood wiping his free hand carefully on his jeans before offering it to Rachel. Rachel elected to take pity on him. "Here, let me hold Todd while you gather up the—no, that wouldn't work. Small children hate to go to strangers. He'd probably cry even harder."

Daniel looked doubtful. "I don't think that's possible.

Rachel laughed. "Maybe not, although he does seem to be winding down a bit. I know he just had a scare, but I was watching you come down the block and he was already crying before you took your spill. What's the problem? Is he tired? Is it naptime?"

Daniel's eyes widened as he stared at her. Could it be that simple? For a man who'd effortlessly flown through school and his first accounting job while maintaining, if he said so himself, a, um, satisfying social life, he'd crashed big-time with the entry of Todd into his life. Daniel knew next to nothing about children. Truth be told, he was rapidly developing an inferiority complex—something he'd never suffered from in the past. "He's been unhappy for the last hour and I haven't got a clue. You know anything about little kids?" he questioned eagerly.

Rachel shrugged in surprise. God, his eyes were blue. Through dint of sheer will, she managed to respond to his question. "I had one that I managed to get through this stage without inadvertently killing him," she admitted. "But it was a long time ago. Mark's eighteen now." And gone away to college. She'd be lucky if she heard from him once a week. He'd probably join a fraternity and stay out drinking all night. He'd insisted on a coed dorm. What if his roommate had girls in till all hours? What if *Mark* had girls in till—

Daniel interrupted her worn-out thought pattern. "You think putting him to bed would make the crying stop? I thought maybe he was hungry since I was starting to feel a few hunger pains myself."

Didn't he know his own son's schedule? Rachel eyed the man dubiously, beginning to wonder about Daniel Van Scott. What kind of father was he? Her mother had explained to her once—this was before Ron had come on the scene and taken an interest in Rachel strictly, Rachel was convinced, so her mother could say *I told you so*— that the super good-looking ones weren't always such a great catch. Girls were so grateful when the handsome ones displayed any interest that they never required anything of the hunks but to be seen with them. Now Rachel wished she'd listened to her mother, but who could tell a seventeen-year-old anything?

Who could tell a thirty-seven-year old anything? 'Cause even though Momma's words had already borne fruit once, Handsome here was too darn beautiful to throw back and waste if he wasn't already spoken for. She glanced at the watch on her wrist. "It's one-fifteen now. Todd hasn't eaten lunch yet?"

Daniel shook his head eagerly. "No, that's why we went up to the store. To get some food. You think that's part of the problem, too?"

Rachel eyed him askance while she tried to figure out if he was serious. He certainly appeared sincere. Had Daniel's genetic code worn itself out creating his truly spectacular exterior? "All I know is that if Mark didn't eat by noon and crash in his crib by twelve-thirty every afternoon, all hell would break loose. Hungry, tired babies are cranky and decidedly unfun individuals to be around."

Daniel suddenly felt reenergized. This woman was a godsend. He'd pick her brains and maybe he wouldn't have to wade through all the child care books he'd bought yesterday. Galvanized into action he thrust Todd at Rachel. "Here, you hold him for a minute while I throw this stuff back into the wagon. I thought he'd like the ride up to the store and back. Boy, was I ever wrong. He wouldn't even stay seated in the wagon. I'm amazed we made it this far without a major catastrophe."

"He's not going to come to a stranger," Rachel argued, leaving Todd dangling between them. "Why don't you let me run upstairs for a washcloth so you can clean yourself up and some empty bags and then I'll pick this stuff up while you cuddle him? Your bags ripped when the wagon turned over."

"Listen," Daniel said, still holding Todd out to her even though Rachel's arms remained at her side. "You're no more a stranger to him than I am."

She should have minded her own business. She should have stayed up in that new empty-feeling apartment of hers and sulked for a few more days. Who cared if she never met her new neighbors? This one at least, was obviously a weirdo. She questioned him suspiciously. "How can you be a stranger to your own son? You're not one of those people you read about who are divorced and kidnap their own children, are you?"

Daniel set Todd against Rachel's chest and propped him there with one hand while he reached down with the other and grabbed her arm. He brought it up and wrapped it around Todd's back before letting go.

Rachel looked down at her arm in surprise then at Daniel, then back at her arm. It had tingled when he'd

touched her to make her hold—what was his name?—
Todd. That kind of electrical impulse upon contact sort
of thing hadn't happened to her since early high school.
How bizarre. If it hadn't been August and humid as all
get-out, Rachel would have been convinced Daniel had
been scuffing his feet and had zapped her with static
electricity.

Her eyes narrowed. No wonder he knew nothing
about caring for small children. If Daniel could do that
to a relative stranger, he'd probably fried his wife's brain
out making love to her ages ago. No doubt she was
nothing but a shell of her former self by now, unable to
think for herself and doing anything and everything
Daniel bid. How disgusting.

Daniel, meanwhile, began to grab cans and toss them
haphazardly into the wagon as quickly as he could. He'd
never realized how freeing it was to have two hands for
a task—not until two days ago. "Don't be silly. I've
never been married in my life. I lived with a girl briefly
right out of college, but nothing permanent came of it,
certainly not a child."

Rachel cringed as Daniel flipped the apples in after the
cans. Didn't he know they'd be so bruised from the
rough treatment as to be inedible? "Todd's not yours
then?"

Daniel straightened and wiped his forehead with the
inside of his arm. "He is now." He stood and absent-
mindedly brushed his hands off on his pants, then
grimaced as the grit-embedded scrapes on his palms
made contact with the fabric. Thoughtfully he examined the gift from God in front of him. The woman—
Rachel, wasn't it?—had shifted Todd onto one softly
padded hip and gently bounced him there. For the first
time in forty-eight hours the child looked—if not happy,

close enough to it for government work. He'd definitely stopped wailing and was staring, fascinated at Rachel's silken tresses. Daniel snapped his fingers and pointed. "It's the right color," he said.

Rachel frowned at him as she twisted her head to one side to keep Todd from reaching her hair and pulling it. "What is?"

"Your hair."

"The right color for what?"

"For Todd. It's the right color for Todd," Daniel said, apropos of nothing as far as Rachel could determine. Evidently he'd burnt out his own brain as well as his former girlfriend's.

"Fine," she said, determined to hand Todd back to Daniel and get out of there. The child was absolutely darling—when he wasn't yodeling at top volume, but as far as Rachel could tell, the situation was rapidly deteriorating. So much for meeting the new neighbors. She'd think long and hard before getting involved with strangers—emphasis on strange—next time.

Daniel took a step backward while shaking his head. He wasn't taking Todd back on a bet. Not while this woman with the magic touch was here. "Listen, just carry him down three houses. That's not so much, is it? Just three houses. Keep showing him your hair, it's just like his mother's was."

Was? Past tense? Rachel looked down on the child in her arms with newfound empathy. "If he accidentally gets a hold of it, he'll pull it out," she warned.

And that would be a shame, Daniel couldn't help thinking. Rachel had gorgeous dark sable hair shot through with threads of some very light color. She wore it shoulder length, turned under in a gentle bob. Under ordinary circumstances he'd—but no, these were not ordinary circumstances. He couldn't afford to digress or get distracted—some things transcended mere incidentals like bald spots on otherwise beautiful women. "I'll buy you a wig," he promised, then rashly went on, "I'll buy you anything you want if you'll just stick with me for the next half hour or so."

The man was pathetic, Rachel decided then and there. Absolutely, totally, one hundred percent pathetic. It was her moral responsibility, her civic duty even, to make sure this poor child happily tugging on the extremely low carat gold chain around her neck—whomever he belonged to—was fed, changed and put down for a humor-restoring nap.

Daniel read her wavering in her eyes. Wanting to consolidate any ground he might have just gained, he decided to start walking. She'd have to follow, wouldn't she? What would he do if she didn't? He was a desperate, desperate man. It would be a mistake—a sign of weakness to turn and look. Daniel pulled the wagon another two feet. He couldn't stand it. He turned and looked anyway. Rachel was reluctantly following. Todd still straddled her hip and he was still complaining, but the greatly lowered volume showed that the sincerity of the complaints was now in serious question. "Thank you," he breathed. "Thank you very much." The first was directed to the heavens, the second to the angel in human disguise following him down the sidewalk.

Rachel stepped up onto the front stoop of the corner brick bungalow and waited for Daniel to unlock the door. It had been a long time ago and she'd been a younger woman when she'd last carted a heavy toddler around in her arms. They ached and she wished Daniel would hurry. Finally he got the door opened. Daniel's

manners at least couldn't be faulted. He held it while she
preceded him over the threshold.

"This is nice," Rachel said as she took in the decorating with surprise. Not that it was totally feminine—
although a woman's touch was evident—it just wasn't
ultramasculine. No sofa made of leather cushions slung
over shiny metal frames. No ultramodern framed
graphics on the wall. And no heavy generic male-on-his-
own brown and black against white walls color scheme.

Where was Daniel's bachelor-on-the-loose decorating statement? And where, oh where, did Todd fit in to
all this?

This house screamed of a married couple, not a single dad. It was a home Rachel could be comfortable in,
decorating she might have chosen herself. Cream painted
walls with cream-colored sheers and window scarves
softened the views of the street. A sofa and love seat at
right angles to each other were done in an eye-pleasing
sherbet-toned tapestry fabric. Both pieces sat in front of
a fireplace with a beautiful carved stone mantel and
surround.

Rachel shook her head in bemusement. Daniel didn't
seem like the type to collect antique lace and have it
framed on sherbet-colored matt boards. And the dusty
rose carpet set off the sofa and accessories to perfection, but—well, suffice it to say no man *she* knew would
have ordered it. Weirder and weirder still.

"The kitchen's through here," Daniel said, taking the
lead.

Rachel followed. "Did you, um, have somebody do
the decorating for you?" And did you pay the bill after
you saw what they'd done?

"What? Oh, my sister did the decorating. She even
reupholstered the sofa herself. I still can't believe it. All

that work and for what—?" Daniel shook his head, grief
and sadness showing briefly in his eyes before determi-
nation once again glinted there. "Here's the high chair."

Gratefully Rachel tucked her burden into the seat and
fastened the lap strap before pushing the tray snuggly
against his little baby potbelly. She rolled her shoulders
in relief. "Okay, so what did you buy to feed monster
man here?" Rachel asked.

"Hot dogs," Daniel announced. "Hot dogs and
cheese. What kid could turn up his nose at that?" With
a flourish he reached into the bottom of a bag, which
was ripped down both sides, and handed her the plastic
shrink-wrapped packages of hot dogs and a brick of
cheese.

And he couldn't have figured out Todd was hungry?
"They have bite marks in them," she said. "Both packages. Right through the plastic."

"Yeah, well Todd's got a real long arm reach for such
a little kid. When he gets older I'm going to look into
basketball camp for him, I think. Natural-born ball
stealer, I bet. He got a hold of them and put up such a
fuss every time I tried to take one away, the lady at the
checkout told me not to bother. Said she'd seen it before. In fact, she acted like she thought it was kind of
funny."

"I'm sure she did," Rachel responded drolly as she
unwrapped the cheese and began to cut it into itsy bitsy
cubes a toddler couldn't choke on. "After all, it wasn't
her kid sucking on a wrapper that's been handled or
sneezed on by eight thousand unknown food handlers
and shoppers with colds. Got a bib?"

Daniel blanched at that while he reached into a
drawer. "Here. Maybe that's what's wrong with him.
He's sick. Maybe I should call the pediatrician."

Rachel snapped the bib around Todd's neck, took the hot dog out of Daniel's hand and began to dice it up. "I doubt it. Not that fast. Here, put this in the microwave and heat it up, but not too hot. Are there any vegetables we can give him?"

"Uh, yeah, sure. I think I saw a can of beans here someplace . . . here we go."

Todd was stuffing bits of cheese into his mouth as fast as he could. He banged his fist on the tray and laughed when more went flying into the air. Rachel took the plate with the dismembered hot dog on it out of the microwave when it beeped and shoveled that onto the tray. Then she found a small handled cup and filled it with half an inch of milk. This, too, she gave the boy. Thirstily Todd drained it with only a small portion dribbling down his chin. Rachel gave him another half inch in the bottom of the cup before going to work on the beans.

Daniel was impressed. "Wow, you're like an old hand at this."

"It's probably like riding a bicycle," Rachel replied, knowing Todd was done when he began to throw the food on the floor. She began the washup procedure. "It's been a while, but it does seem to be coming back to me." Rachel held Todd's cup up in front of the boy. "Look, Todd. This is your cup. See? Your cup is yellow."

"Lellow."

Rachel smiled, pleased. "That's right. Yellow. Where's his bedroom?" she asked Daniel.

Daniel pointed. "Right through there."

She nodded. "Okay. How about if you finish cleaning up in here? I'll change his diapers and see if I can get him settled down." Feeling only slightly guilty—after all, it wasn't her child who'd made the mess, was it?—Rachel left the kitchen area and headed for the nursery. There, she found a box of disposable diapers and replaced Todd's soggy one and played with his toes briefly while he lay on the changing table.

"This little piggy went to market—" The room had been lovingly prepared by someone who hadn't wanted to know the sex of their child beforehand. Someone who liked surprises had chosen a lovely but nonsexist pale lime tint for the walls. The woodwork was a crisp contrasting white.

"This little piggy stayed home—" A border of rainbows hung up high where the walls met the ceiling. Did Daniel ever stop and point them out to Todd?

"This little piggy had roast beef—" A big, fat, stuffed fabric rainbow splayed itself across the wall next to the crib. She'd used a similar theme in Mark's nursery, Rachel remembered. Impossible as it seemed, it had been nineteen years ago when she'd decorated that nursery. Nineteen years. Rachel had been eighteen, practically a baby herself, she now realized.

Rachel sighed. "This little piggy had none—" She reminded herself that she was done being melancholy as of that morning.

"And this little piggy cried—"

Daniel popped his head in the doorway. "All cleaned up. How's it going in here?"

"Wee, wee, wee all the way home." Rachel brushed the bottom of Todd's foot with a light ticklish motion and smiled when Todd grinned up at her and jerked his foot back. She picked up his other foot and blew a raspberry on the bottom of it. That got a laugh. Finally Rachel looked up. "Fine. I'm going to rock him for a minute to settle him down before I put him in the crib."

"Fine, great, whatever. You get me a couple of hours of peace and quiet and I'll be your slave forever."

Rachel snorted at that. "Yeah, right." But it was an interesting idea. A body like that, her slave? My, oh my. That certainly got the old heart valves pumping. She picked Todd up and noticed a framed birth announcement hung on the wall. Todd Michael *Malone?* Sarah and Michael Malone proudly announce the birth of their son, Todd Michael? "Daniel, *who* does Todd really belong to? Are you baby-sitting for a relative or something?" She'd just die if Eileen turned out right once again. But this Sarah and Michael must have been really hard up to leave their pride and joy with a man who knew next to nothing about children.

But Daniel's indulgent smile immediately disappeared. His face tightened. "Todd's mother, Sarah, was my sister. Her husband won a cruise as a prize in a sales contest where he worked. It was the first time they'd ever left the baby." Daniel sighed. "There was a fire on board the ship. Barely big enough to make the papers up here, but Sarah, Michael and a couple of other passengers died of smoke inhalation. Todd stayed with Mike's parents while I got my own life straightened out, but they're well into their seventies and in a retirement complex with no children allowed. My mother has Alzheimer's. Caring for her takes up all my dad's time. That leaves Todd and me as a team."

Rachel gaped at him as she seated herself in the rocker. And she'd thought *she'd* had troubles. "Oh. I'm so sorry. How awful."

Daniel ran a hand back through his hair. "Yeah, well, it's been a little rocky the past couple of days, I have to admit.'' He eyed the picture Rachel made there in the rocker with Todd happily sucking his thumb while resting his head on her shoulder. "But I think maybe God just opened a window."

Chapter Two

Rachel continued to stare at him. "Excuse me?" she finally said while absently rubbing Todd's little back. His body already felt half limp. Another minute or two and he'd be conked out cold.

"I said—"

"Shh, not so loud. He's almost asleep."

It was comical how quickly Daniel lowered his voice. Now she could barely hear him. "You know the old saying about God always opening a window when he closes a door?" he whispered.

Warily Rachel nodded.

"Well, when Sarah and Michael died, that was a heavy-duty door to get slammed in poor Todd's face." Daniel leaned against the nursery door frame and raked his hand through his hair. "*I'm* sure not the open window. I'm trying as hard as I can, but all I remember of parenting is that my dad used to play ball with me. Todd's too little to *throw* a baseball let alone catch one.

It was a disaster when I tried the other day. The ball kept going right through his legs.''

Rachel arched a brow at him in disbelief. He hadn't really pitched a baseball at a toddler, had he?

Daniel continued, "The thing is, right before this all happened I'd just quit the accounting firm I'd been with since graduating from college. I was all set to go out on a limb and out on my own. Do you know how much work that entails? The time commitment? I've got to get this thing set up and going—make it viable or Todd and I are cooked geese. There'll be no income. I want to save the insurance money for his college fund. Even if I could take a crash course in child raising and was instantly expert at it, I haven't got the time to lavish on him the way he needs and deserves, do you understand what I mean? I can't stick him in day-care now. For crying out loud, as far as he's concerned both his parents just deserted him. What does he understand about death? So what am I supposed to do? I'm no Mr. Mom."

Todd snored gently in her ear. Rachel slowly rose and walked quietly over to the crib. She eased the boy off her shoulder and laid him in his bed. She picked the blanket with the satin binding to lightly cover him and made sure he'd be able to feel that comforting edging against his cheek and hand while he slept. Daniel followed right behind as she crept from the room. He spoke his next words as softly as the rest, but he might as well have shouted, they jarred her so.

"If God's trying to open a window for Todd, it sure as all heck ain't me. I barely constitute a crack in the glass or a missing piece of weather stripping. So I have to ask myself, Where's the open window?" Then he sort of studied her out of the corner of his eye.

Oh, no. *Oh, no.* The last time she'd let some fast-talking male open her window, it had been eighteen years before she'd managed to get it shut again, and even then it hadn't been without a kick start from her supposed loving husband—the very one who'd insisted on opening the damn thing in the first place. Uh-uh. No way was she going to go through any of that again, although he was absolutely right about one thing, Rachel thought as she walked as quickly as possible back down the hallway. Daniel Van Scott was definitely cracked.

Daniel followed her closely. "Don't you think it's a little bit odd you picked that exact moment to look out your window? You could have just as easily been, I don't know, in the kitchen or the bathroom. Even in the living room, for crying out loud, but with your back to the window. You fit into this equation somehow, I just know it."

"No," Rachel stated emphatically, knowing she needed to be firm here. She did not like the way this conversation was headed. She was done with being dutiful. It was now officially her turn to play in the sun. Being footloose and fancy-free was supposed to be one of the few advantages of the empty nest stage. "I hate to be the stereotypical female, but I was never much good at math. Especially quadratic equations. They always threw me for a loop."

Daniel caught Rachel's arm and halted her flight. He thought fast. "All right. Okay. You probably work and can't help me out yourself. But you've got a real way with little kids. Maybe you know somebody else with your knack?"

Rachel stopped and looked up at him. Those blue eyes of his were killers, especially the way they appeared now, both serious and sincere. She was in big-time trouble here and she was just bright enough to know it. She was not about to disabuse him of his faulty notion that she worked. "Daniel, what is it that you want from me?"

"Help," he stated simply. "Either yours or somebody you could recommend. I know I haven't known you long, but somehow I feel like I can trust you. I'm dying here."

Her arm tingled where he touched it. Rachel knew it without a shadow of a doubt. That spark she felt was plain old sexual attraction, no getting around it. You'd have thought that by thirty-seven her body would have forgotten all about that special tingle. It was discouraging, downright undignified that it hadn't. Imagine, at her age she was being suckered in by a pair of broad shoulders, blue eyes and a sob story that had absolutely nothing to do with her. If she didn't get out of there, she'd do something stupid—like agreeing to do what he wanted whether it was in her own best interest or not. Shades of the past! This was ridiculous. It was mortifying. It was an insult to her intelligence. Hadn't she learned *anything* over the past eighteen years? "Daniel, no one comes to mind off the top of my head, but I'll think about it and call you if I come up with a name. But for now, I've got to get going. All those boxes aren't going to unpack themselves, you know." There was a hint of desperation in her voice and she hoped Daniel didn't pick up on it.

He ran his hand up her arm and her arm broke out in goose pimples. Eighty degrees outside, and she had *goose bumps,* oh, *puh-leeze!*

"Rachel, don't leave yet. Let me at least give you lunch. Come on, have a hot dog with me. It's the least I can do."

Rachel thought about those hot dogs with the bite marks she'd fixed for Todd. He was right. It was the very least he could do. "I don't know—"

"Please?"

Oh well, what did she have at home? Low fat peanut butter and reduced sugar strawberry jam. Yummy. "Oh, all right."

"Great! Good! Come on back to the kitchen."

Daniel's smile lit his face and Rachel knew without a doubt she'd just made a grave tactical error. She hadn't agreed to anything other than lunch, darn it. Daniel's problems were his. Rachel had enough of her own without borrowing more. She'd just have to keep telling herself that until she'd choked down her premasticated hot dog. Maybe she could still get out of there relatively unscathed.

Daniel steered her back into the kitchen and pulled out a chair at the round oak kitchen table. "Here. You sit down. I'll handle this."

Rachel refused to feel badly about letting him. For too many years she'd had meals waiting on the table and clean socks and underwear in her men's drawers. For what? Her son had eagerly left for college without even a backward glance and shortly thereafter her husband had just plain left. Besides, anybody could boil a hot dog.

Even Daniel. Within a very few minutes he served her up a plate with not only the promised main course, but apple sauce and potato chips. Then he really went all out and dug the mustard and pickle relish out of the refrigerator as well. He poured her a glass of milk. Rachel couldn't remember the last time she'd drunk milk. Oh well, at her age wasn't osteoporosis just around the corner? Maybe the milk would hold it at bay a little while longer. Surprisingly Rachel enjoyed the meal. "This is good," she told him, touched that he'd taken the trouble to find her a hot dog Todd hadn't sampled in the store.

"Thank you," Daniel said, and smiled at her praise.

His grin almost blinded her. Rachel quickly lowered her head and studied the mustard smear on her plate. So much for that conversational gambit. "Well, I guess I ought to—"

Daniel jumped up and grabbed the plates off the table, startling her. "No need to rush," he said. He suddenly realized he was starving for a little adult conversation. How did young mothers do this all day every day? He glanced at the watch bound to his wrist. "Rachel, how long do you think Todd will be out?"

"What? Oh, if he's anything like Mark, maybe two hours."

"Two hours," he repeated after her and his face assumed an expression similar to the one she wore when she came face-to-face with a piece of maple fudge with her name on it. "That's fantastic, two whole hours. I can get a lot done in one hundred and twenty uninterrupted minutes. Let's see, first I'll dump in a load of laundry real quick like. Let's say, oh, ten minutes for that, another fifteen for these dishes. That leaves—hey, I just might have enough time to get my computer and maybe even the printer set up before Todd rejoins the land of the living. I can't do it when he's up, you know. That kid is murder on floppy disks."

She believed it. Rachel remembered this stage all too well. "I really should be going. I've got boxes of my own—"

"Oh, that's right. I wish you could stick around. It would be nice to talk to another adult for a while."

Daniel shrugged philosophically. "But if you can't, you can't. I really appreciate everything you did do for me this afternoon, though, Rachel. I want to be sure you know that."

Rachel had never realized it before, but evidently she really was a sucker for blue eyes. Ron had had blue eyes, but not like Daniel's blue eyes. It would be very easy to make a fool of herself with this man. It would be no hardship at all to talk herself into spending the afternoon talking to Daniel while he set up his office. Heck, she'd probably even pitch in and help. *When* would she learn?

Rachel told herself she was simply in the middle of a major empty nest syndrome crisis in her own life. That's why she wanted to adopt these two. Fill the nest back up. She was just a natural born caretaker, a nurturer.

Natural born masochist was more like it.

But no, she'd get through this thing on her own, without any placebos. It was simply a case of hardening her heart and walking out his front door. She'd already done more than any other woman who'd come across that scene she'd witnessed out on her front sidewalk would have—well, maybe not, considering Daniel's shoulders and butt—but still, she'd done her corporal work of mercy. "You're more than welcome," she said. "But now I've really got to go."

With that, Rachel made her escape. There wasn't a shadow of doubt in her mind that it had been a close one, too.

Rachel spent her afternoon organizing her cupboards. She unpacked her silverware and placed it all neatly in a new silver separator she'd bought for the drawer closest to the sink drain board. Then she stacked the dishes in the cabinet up above the silverware and the

pots and pans—what few she needed to cook for one—
in the cabinet below the rangetop.

By the time she broke for dinner, Rachel was out in the
hall and mostly done with unwrapping the new linens
she'd bought for her fresh start in life. The linen closet
looked good, she decided as she stepped back and examined it. Towels that actually coordinated not only
with each other but the bathroom as well, sat folded in
the same direction and in neat piles on the shelf in front
of her. Combined with the sheets, blankets and pillows
she'd bought, it looked like a well-done department store
display, Rachel thought.

She took another step back. It appeared just the way
she'd always wanted her old linen closet to look and the
way it would have looked if she'd ever gotten any co-
operation from her son and former husband. But no,
they'd always rooted through her neat piles and then
walked off, leaving the disaster behind them. Well, no
more. This closet would win homemaking awards—only
there was nobody left to make a home for. Again Rachel lectured herself. "Buck up. You can't win any
homemaking awards if there are people living in the
house. It's just one of life's poorer jokes. Oh well,
maybe Mark will come home for winter and spring
break. Possibly even part of the summer. He can mess
up the towels then." She hoped so, but basically Rachel
just had to recognize she was all alone now. That was
simply the way it was. Her stack of towels would remain neat forevermore.

On that rather melancholy note, Rachel returned to
her small kitchen and baked a frozen, premade chicken
potpie and pulled a handful of salad out of a pretossed
bag of greens.

She ate it all by herself with nothing but the radio for company. Rachel wondered what Daniel and Todd were eating for dinner. More hot dogs?

Rachel washed her plate and fork and set them on the drain board. Her days of needing a dishwasher were over, she mused as she contemplated the lonely utensils. The phone rang as she turned away from the sink.

"Mom? It's me, Mark."

Alarm bells rang in Rachel's maternal mind. "Mark? What's wrong?"

"Chill out, Mom. Nothing's wrong. I just wanted to see what was going down on the maternal home front. You know, see how you were doing and stuff."

Rachel barely controlled her snort of disbelief. Yeah, right. In other words, her best beloved son wanted something from her. "I'm fine, Mark, just fine. I spent the day organizing my new apartment and guess what?"

"What?"

"It's been four whole hours since I put the silverware away and it's all still in the right compartments! No teaspoons mixed in with the soup spoons, no forks stuck up so the drawer can't close, no knives left with the cutting edge up. It's like a miracle, Mark, an honest to God miracle."

"Very funny, Mom. When the guys here ask about my parents, one of the first things I mention is my mother's great sense of humor. Of course then I have to break it to them that you still use snail mail because you are, like, the most totally computer illiterate person I know and couldn't use e-mail if your life depended on it. It wrecks the image, Mom, like totally destroys it."

Rachel laughed. "You'll be happy to know I'm thinking about taking a computer class."

That surprised her son. "Really? What for?"

"So I can get a job. Gotta support myself now, you know. Dad only pays alimony for the next six months. After that I'm supposed to be back on my feet and self-supporting."

Mark's response sounded disconcerted, as though they'd strayed into territory he'd just as soon avoid. "Oh, yeah. Right. That, um, sucks. So, uh, what else is happening?"

Rachel understood her son's reluctance to be caught up in adult problems. She thought back over her day. Really, only one item of import stuck in her mind. "I met a guy," she reported. "He's going to try to raise his little nephew all by himself. He crashed his nephew's little red wagon right in front of my new place. The little boy was crying and groceries were everywhere. I had to go out and save them. Todd—that's the child—is a little pistol, but Daniel—that's the guy—seemed real nice. Sincere, but in over his head, if you know what I mean."

"A guy with a wagon? Sounds like a dork."

"He's not a dork!" God, no. Daniel Van Scott was anything but dorky. Oh, man, here it was hours later and Rachel got the shivers just thinking about him. She was going to give herself high blood pressure if she didn't watch out. End up on medication like her mother, for crying out loud. "He just tripped, that's all."

"Like I said, sounds like a dork."

"Well, he's not." Not by a long shot. "Now, what's new with you, Mark? Your classes going okay? You're studying enough? Are you meeting any nice girls?" Ones that still go to church?

Her son's voice came back sounding entirely too casual for a mother's peace of mind. "Yeah, I've met a few. Most of them are sorority tools, if you know what

I mean, but this one's pretty cool. She's vegetarian. I had no idea meat was so totally bad for you and the environment, too. I'm never eating it again, man.''

Oh, God. ''Mark, how will you get enough protein in your diet? How will you—''

''Chill out, Mom. I'll be fine. But what I need is one of those small refrigerators for my room. You know, so I can keep yogurt and stuff like that on hand.''

Rachel walked into her living room with the cordless phone and sank into the sofa. She tucked her feet up underneath herself. ''So go get one.''

''*Mooom.*''

Her son's disembodied voice came back at her and she had no trouble imagining the despairing look on his face.

''They're *expensive,* you know? I'd need like, eighty or ninety dollars put into my checking account. Think you could do that for me?''

Ah, they'd reached the crux of the phone call. Money. She'd been warned about this from friends with older children. ''Mark, you had three hundred dollars when your father and I dropped you off at school just a very short time ago.''

''Yeah, but I bought this totally awesome game for my computer and I had to have a good bike for getting around campus 'cuz nobody uses the campus bus, so I turned in the pass you guys bought me and spent the cash on a bike helmet, you'll be glad to know. And I bought this unbelievable mountain bike. It was on sale and everything, so how could I go wrong?''

Rachel put her hand over her eyes and collapsed back into the sofa. ''You've already gone through all your money? Mark, that should have lasted you a couple of months!''

"How was I supposed to know something else would come up that I'd need?" Mark asked, his logic clear, at least in his own mind. "I mean, you should see the graphics on this computer game I got. It was going to be my entertainment for the semester. But now, with this girl and all, she'll probably want to go to the movies and stuff. And I really need that refrigerator—actually, a small microwave would be cool, too. A lot of the guys here have them. And at least I'm better than my roommate. He never takes his girlfriend anywhere! All they do is fool around. One of these nights that top bunk is going to crash right down on top of me—probably kill me."

Rachel just about collapsed. "Your roommate and his girlfriend are... doing *that* while you're in the room?" she squeaked. Oh, God. Oh God, oh God, oh God.

Mark paused in his spiel, evidently aware he may have gone too far. "Well, yeah, but it's no big deal," he quickly assured his mother. "I mean, you probably can't remember back to when you were interested in sex, but it's pretty normal for my age group, you know."

Oh God, oh God, oh God. She should have had a talk with Mark before he'd left for school. She should have bought him some condoms, made sure they'd gotten into his suitcase. She'd gotten pregnant with Mark on prom night, her senior year in high school. It had been her first foray into the mysterious world of male-female—looking back on it, boy-girl—sex stuff. It had changed the direction of her entire life and Mark was only a few months past that point in his life. He needed at least another three or four years before he took a chance like that. It could change your life completely. Rachel knew.

She'd given Mark an eleven-thirty curfew on his prom night. Ron had smirked, but Rachel had been unwilling to take any chances. Was Mark making up for lost opportunities now?

And her son didn't think she remembered the pull of sexual feelings? All she had to do was think about the rush she'd gotten just looking at Daniel Van Scott this afternoon and Rachel knew she wasn't dead yet. Not by a long shot.

Mark cleared his throat. "Uh, Mom, you still there?"

Maybe, maybe not. This could all be some kind of strange out-of-body type experience. She wasn't really having this bizarre phone conversation with her own, carefully raised son. "Mark, I'm afraid you're going to have to talk to your father," Rachel heard herself say. "Going through all your spending money in a little over a week was a choice you made. I guess as far as I'm concerned, my feeling is now you have to live with that decision. Either that or get a part-time job. At any rate, it's something you'll have to deal with.

"By the way, I found some of your old Tonka trucks when I was packing. I couldn't help keeping them when your dad and I cleaned out the old house. I was thinking I'd give them to that little boy I was telling you about. He's the perfect age for them."

"What? You're giving away my Tonkas? Not on your life. I still want those. That kid'll just have to get his own toy trucks. Those are mine."

Rachel shook her head and tried to organize her thoughts. Her collegiate, urbane son who talked about sex ever so casually refused to be parted from his toy trucks. Life was strange. Her son was strange. Heck, in all probability, *she* was strange. "Mark, I'm hanging up now. Let me know if you have any luck with your dad and call me again some time. But just to talk, you know?

It would be nice to hear from you when you didn't necessarily need something from me.''

Rachel hung up the phone after a series of motherly admonishments about studying hard and making sure he kept his new bicycle tethered with a lock through the bike's frame, not just the tire. She thought about broaching safe sex, but Mark cut her off, which, when the phone call was all done, left her pacing the living room.

"Now I know how my own mother felt," she muttered to the walls as she circled the room. "This is like a nightmare and he hasn't even gotten anybody pregnant yet!" Maybe she should go out in the morning and by a box of condoms. Send them to him, just in case.

For some reason, condom shopping brought to mind Daniel and the idea hit that maybe she could confiscate a few out of the box before she sent it and keep them for herself.

"Don't be ridiculous," Rachel immediately chastised herself. "The poor man's got his hands full without having to deal with your midlife sexual identity crisis as well." Again she circled the room, gesturing with big sweeping movements of her hands as she lectured. "Besides, didn't you learn anything from your experience with Ron? For crying out loud, the man talks you into bed—well, actually the grass in that corner of the football field under the scoreboard, but that's just details—gets you pregnant, graciously marries you so you can work your fingers, hands, heck, your *arms* to the bone putting him through school and then the jerk sticks around barely long enough to get the kid out the door, before clearing out himself so fast I'm surprised he didn't get something vital caught in the door when it swung shut after Mark." Rachel paused and thought about that. "Actually it's kind of too bad he didn't."

She shook her hand in the air. "Anyway, whatever, the point is, I thought we'd made our marriage work. Yes, it had gotten off to a rough start, but I thought we'd worked through all that and made it. What a fool I was. I don't want Mark to have to get married, have this carry on to the second generation. And certainly, *certainly* I couldn't live through it a second time myself."

And Daniel Van Scott was simply too attractive for her peace of mind. Right then and there, Rachel made a vow to keep her distance. There was some kind of very odd, no doubt, chemical attraction at play here. She hadn't felt it, well, in eighteen years, and she'd at least managed to convince herself it had been true love rather than adolescent hormones back then. She no longer wore the blinders of youth, and in a way, it hurt.

No, there was no point in making a fool of herself a second time.

Rachel slept, but not well. In the morning, she cooked a single egg and matched it up with a solitary piece of toast. She washed the one plate she'd dirtied, then took herself out for a walk to explore her new neighborhood. There was a small park a block and a half up. Rachel could see a bank of stores another block after that.

Rachel glanced at the park once more and thought. The sun was shining, the few clouds in the sky were on the run, and although it was September now, summer was still in the air. She walked up to the stores and bought a paperback novel at the drugstore and a foam cup of take-out coffee at the corner restaurant. Carting both items back to the park, Rachel made herself comfortable on a green wooden bench. Most of the toddlers surrounding her were happily playing and provided a

pleasant white noise while she basked in the warm sun
and read her book.

"Hey, what's this, another day off? Or do you work
nights?"

Rachel instantly knew who had settled on the bench
next to her. That low-timbred voice had played a major
part in her restlessness last night. "Hi, Daniel," she said.
"I assumed you'd be spending the morning getting your
office set up."

"Hey, Todd, no pushing. That other little boy was on
the horsey first. You'll have to wait your turn." Daniel
yawned and draped his arms along the bench back.

The tips of his fingers were very close to touching
Rachel's shoulders and she'd never been more aware of
a man. Not even when she'd been sixteen.

"I got up early," Daniel admitted, more pleased than
he was comfortable with to find Rachel in the park.
"Worked for a couple of hours before the champ woke
up. I found a playpen in the back of his closet and set it
up in the study. He played pretty happily in there for a
little while, too. I figured we both deserved a break before lunch. I'll get more done during his nap. Did you see
that kid hit Todd? Where's his mother? Why isn't she
watching that monster more closely?"

"Todd took his truck."

"Oh, well, uh, *Todd*," Daniel called out, "*give the
little boy's toy back*. I guess next time I better bring a
couple of our own sand toys for him, huh?"

Rachel shrugged more casually than she was feeling.
"You seem to be getting the feeling for this pretty
quickly. It sounds like you managed just fine this morning."

Daniel stretched his legs out in front of him, crossing them at the ankle. He gave an expansive, contented sigh. "Yeah. I even had a couple of inquiries already from former clients who knew I was going out on my own." He gave Rachel a sidelong glance. He must have been more harried than he'd thought yesterday. This woman was positively beautiful. And he hadn't noticed? He was slipping, definitely slipping. But she was here now and so was he. He—

"Really? That's terrific."

"Yeah, I just wish I could get my system up a bit faster so I could get some estimates out to people, but it'll probably take a few more days. *No, Todd, keep your shoes on. There might be broken glass or sharp stones in the grass.*" After that admonishment, Daniel turned his head and studied Rachel through narrowed eyes. Whoa. Nice eyes. Big and a gorgeous warm brown. "You on vacation?"

Rachel cleared her throat. "Well, actually I'm sort of between positions at the moment, I guess you could say." Was she ever.

Daniel perked up at that. Maybe persistence could pay off? "Yeah? Well, I haven't had time to get an ad into the paper, let alone have anyone answer it. I know you said you didn't want to take a job baby-sitting Todd full time, but what about a kind of temporary thing? You know, help me out until I can get somebody else. When you can, of course. It doesn't have to be forty hours a week or anything. I'd appreciate whatever help I can get. Like this afternoon, if you're not busy I could pay you to get my filing cabinets set up while I try to hook up my new printer. I wasn't able to get to it yesterday."

He looked at her so hopefully, and once the full force of those sky blue eyes was turned on her, Rachel knew she was lost. She'd probably agree to sell her own grandmother if Daniel asked her to. She took a sip of her coffee and burnt the roof of her mouth. Great. Just terrific. Well, might as well get this over with. "I might come down after lunch. For a couple of hours during Todd's nap," she cautiously allowed. Cautious? Hah! Rachel began to despair whether she knew the meaning of the word.

Daniel was no fool. He cemented the deal quickly, before she had any opportunity to change her mind. "Great!" Then, evidently afraid to let her out of his sight, he hastened to offer, "You could eat lunch with us, if you wanted. I was going to make grilled cheeses."

Oh, no. Rachel was determined to limit her exposure to Todd's sunny smiles and cute toddler ways. Right now, she was bent on damage control and would eat low fat peanut butter and reduced sugar strawberry jam if it killed her. Rachel stood and tossed her foam cup into a nearby dark green metal trash barrel. "Thanks for the offer, but I have a few things to do before I come down." Like sit down and weep for a while over her own stupidity. "I'll be down around one o'clock or so."

Daniel stood, too, unable to believe his good fortune. This was one fine-looking woman and she obviously had a tender heart. She was going to take pity on him. Daniel, the former lady killer, was both humble and grateful. Also extremely attracted to Rachel, although he knew enough to sit on that. He wasn't about to do anything stupid and scare her off. "One o'clock. I really appreciate this, Rachel." He snapped his fingers. "Todd will be down by then, so don't ring the doorbell, just knock, okay? Or better yet, I'll leave it unlocked and you can just come right in.''

"Sure, fine,'' Rachel said and waved to Todd as she went to leave the park. But it wasn't fine, not really. Entering a home without knocking bespoke a certain intimacy Rachel would really like to avoid, especially since she seemed so bent on self-destruction.

Chapter Three

Daniel left the park shortly after Rachel. It was still a bit early for lunch, but Todd had decided that dumping fistfuls of sand on top of his head was nothing short of hysterically funny. When the first two explanations of how he could scratch his cornea, possibly go blind, have to go to the hospital and wear a patch over his eye for the rest of his life failed, Daniel packed in the logic. He simply picked the child up, tucked him under his arm and removed his nephew from the source of temptation.

"You're going to regret your precipitous course of action, little buddy," he advised as he strode down the street. "Every bit of that dirt has to come out of your hair before you take your nap. It could still get into your eyes, you know. I wasn't kidding about that patch. At the very least you'll have sand in your bed and you'll hate it." And so would Daniel, who in order to get a peaceful, quiet naptime out of Todd was now going to have to shampoo the little one's head, a thankless task Todd took as a personal affront. Daniel fully expected his eardrums to shatter someday during one of Todd's bath times.

Daniel stood out on his front lawn and held Todd as if he were a football. Todd's body was horizontal and his head projected out in front of Daniel at waist level. Then Daniel ruffled his hand through the tot's hair, gently massaging his scalp as he tried to dislodge as much of the sand as possible before going into the house. Todd thought it was pretty funny and spent his time squirming around as he attempted to grab Daniel's leg and hang upside down and whoop. From that, Daniel assumed he'd managed to keep the gritty particles out of his eyes, thereby successfully avoiding any trips to the emergency room.

"That's about as much as I can take care of out here," he finally told Todd. "We're going to have to hit the tub to get the rest." He went into the house, Todd still tucked under his arm and let the screen slap shut behind him.

"Shoot," he said and reversed himself, reopened the screen and swung Todd upright so he could reach his sneakers. Holding Todd's feet just outside the front door, he pulled off his shoes and dropped them out on the porch into the small pile of sand that had poured out of the offending articles when Daniel had removed them. "Thank God I thought to do that," he muttered as he reentered the house. "I wouldn't want Rachel to see a mess like that inside the house. She'd think I was totally inept." And he never thought to question why he cared one way or the other.

Daniel got thoroughly soaked during Todd's bath and shampoo. All he could think about was how his life had changed in two short months. "I was engaged to be married, made good money, had job security, decent insurance coverage and probably would have made partner by the time I was thirty-five." Daniel shook his head. "How the mighty are fallen." Hard to believe it had only been June when he'd decided to strike out on his own and excitedly so informed his fiancée. He'd thought she'd find it a great adventure—the two of them as a team working their way together, side by side, shoulder to shoulder, through thick and thin—including those lean years that tempered every new business. They'd have eaten a lot of inexpensive pasta and cheap red wine at first, but they'd have done it with panache—by candlelight.

Wrong.

"If Marie couldn't handle the idea of my giving up a secure job with nobody but two adults to worry about feeding, what the heck would she think of this situation?" In retrospect it was obvious Marie had only been interested in him when his future was firmly in place. "But she sure had me fooled for a while there," Daniel admitted as he towel-dried Todd's hair and wriggling little body. "She'd have probably had a heart attack and died if I'd asked her to help out with raising you, you little pill-face."

Todd took the slander with a sunny smile and wrapped his arms around Daniel's neck.

"Hey, lighten up," Daniel protested as he loosened the child's arms. "I'm glad you're starting to adjust, but you're going to choke me."

Todd laughed out loud at that and Daniel rolled his eyes as he carried Todd out to the kitchen and deposited him in the high chair. "Real funny, champ. So funny I forgot to laugh."

Daniel assembled a cheese sandwich and dropped it into a skillet. While it browned, he poured Todd half an inch of milk. Remembering how Rachel had taken pains to describe everything to the child the day before, he said, "Some good white milk, Todd," as he handed the tumbler to the child. "Your milk's in a green cup today. Green, got it?"

Todd gurgled happily. "Geen."

Daniel nodded and turned back to the stove to flip the grilled cheese. "Right, green. And if you dump it over in another ill-advised attempt at not quite two-year-old humor, you're dead meat," he continued under his breath.

Todd banged his cup on his high chair tray and giggled as milk sprayed. Daniel rolled his eyes.

Forty minutes later, Daniel breathed a sigh of relief as he quietly inched the nursery door shut on the napping child. What a difference giving him that satin-bound blanket made. He had to remember to thank Rachel for enlightening him in that respect. It must be one of those universal infant survival tricks that only women seemed to know. Well, he was gradually picking up on the various and sundry survival techniques, but it seemed a slow process to Daniel. However, provided he and Todd didn't kill each other anytime soon, they'd both get through this transition period. Maybe not be the better for it, but at least functioning again.

Just as Daniel was again trying to tell himself what a good thing it was that Marie had abandoned his personal ship, foundering though it was, and how he and Todd were better off without her—they'd caulk their own leaks, trim their own sails just fine, thank you very much—he heard a soft knock on the front door. He listened while the door squealed softly as it was drawn hesitantly open.

"Daniel?" Rachel whispered into the quiet room.

Quickly Daniel made his way down the hall. "Yeah, come on in, Rachel." Every thought of Marie and her perfidy swept right out of his head as he strode forward to intercept Rachel in the living room. One corner of his mouth lifted when he finally had her in his line of vision.

Now there was a *woman*. Just the sight of her in his living room made him smile. Sexy, hell yes, Rachel was certainly that, but also competent and maternal. You didn't see Rachel run at the sound of a screaming child. Toddlers didn't faze Rachel. She took them in her stride. Why, she'd probably be happy, *thrilled* even to help raise a kid with one hand while assisting her man get his business up and running with the other, insurance or no insurance. Between the two of them, they could probably have supper on the table every night at six o'clock even on the most hectic days.

Hmm, now there was a heck of an idea.

"Hi," Rachel said, and knew she was smiling inanely.

She shouldn't have come. She realized it the moment his blue eyes caught hers again, but Daniel moved fast. He had the front door closed behind her and was escorting her into his study before her brain could advise her legs to bolt.

"The study's through here," Daniel said as he guided her.

Rachel's upper arm tingled where his hand rested. Worse, because his hand was tucked *under* her arm as he directed the way, the back of his fingers came very close to brushing the side of her breast. Why, if she was to bring her arm just the tiniest bit in closer to her body, his fingers would . . . God, she was losing her mind.

"I really appreciate your coming," Daniel said in an attempt at conversation when all he could really think about was how his hand could almost encircle her arm. "Just let me move these boxes off my desk chair and you can sit down."

"You don't have to—"

But it was already done. "There, sit."

She sat. It was a tilt chair, the kind you could lean back on and the chair went with you. As Mark would say, awesome. "So what can I do to help you?"

"Frankly all you'd really have to do to make me a happy camper is sit there and talk to me. I have a whole new respect for young mothers. I can't tell you how much I miss simple adult companionship and conversation. I feel like a junkie in need of a fix. Say something, anything, just don't drool or blow spit bubbles while you do it."

Rachel smiled. "Yes, I remember that phase all too well. But look at it this way, it's probably good for you— make you more sympathetic to your wife when you marry."

She wondered at his visible shudder.

"Sorry," Daniel said, "but I just had a rather close call in that department. It's not a subject likely to inspire a lot of happy thoughts for a good long while I'm afraid." Daniel tapped the folders in his hand into the opposite palm thoughtfully. "It's a tough blow to the old ego, I've got to tell you, when you realize the only attraction you held for the woman you thought loved you was that of a meal ticket."

Rachel spun around to face him. "That's what happened to you?"

Daniel continued to pile law briefs into the card-board carton. "Pretty much."

How could anyone look at this man and see nothing but a meal ticket? Rachel wondered. She couldn't imagine how they got past his eyes, for one thing. And if they somehow managed that, how'd they manage not to succumb to those shoulders, to say nothing of his terrific personality? Just look how good he was with Todd, for heaven's sake. Why, whoever the woman was that had hurt Daniel like that must have been a cretin. Sorry, a cretiness, although her femininity was in question as far as Rachel was concerned. "I'm so sorry."

"I'm past it now," Daniel assured Rachel. "A little battle-scarred but the wiser for the experience. Certainly learned a valuable lesson at any rate."

Yes, but had it been the *right* lesson? She had to remind herself that it wasn't her problem. She was out of the child-raising business, out of the male-ego-soothing business. She'd moved on to the next phase of her life, ready or not. A real job in the real working world was next on her list and she would not allow herself to get sidetracked. "Uh, what are you doing?" Rachel asked in a blatant change of topic before things got too heavy.

"Packing up poor Michael's things. I hate to do it, but I need the room. I guess I'll store it all in a corner of the basement. Someday Todd might want to look through his father's stuff." Daniel shrugged helplessly, not at all sure what Todd would do with a bunch of old, dry law briefs in later life, but still unable to get rid of this last remaining connection with his sister and brother-in-law.

Rachel finished with the file folders, rose from the chair and came over to kneel beside him. She sensed how painful a task Daniel had set for himself. "I'll help."

Silently they worked for several minutes together. Gradually a sense of peace stole over Rachel. The inner churning that had probably been burning a hole through her stomach lining ever since Ron had announced he considered their marriage over, actually subsided. It had been such a constant companion these past few months, she almost missed it. Funny how the *absence* of pain could be so noticeable.

In point of fact, Rachel worried about it. She didn't want to find her much-sought-after inner contentment here in this house with Daniel and Todd. She forcibly reminded herself as she neatly slipped books into boxes that it would be incredibly easy to fall back into the old do-anything-to-please patterns. Rachel thought seriously about giving herself a good pinch, just so she wouldn't get too comfortable working there next to Daniel.

"So," Daniel said as he stacked the boxes by the study door. "You said you were between jobs. What were you doing at your last position and what kind of work are you looking for now?" He wasn't just making conversation. Rachel fascinated him. He really wanted to know.

"I worked at home," Rachel explained carefully.

If she thought Daniel would let things go at that, she was woefully mistaken.

"Yeah? Doing what?"

She sighed. "Raising a son and keeping a house so that my former husband could finish his education and get established in a career."

"Oh. I get the feeling the subject is off-limits?"

Rachel went to move her box over by the door with the others, but Daniel beat her to it. Instead she got to watch his biceps bulge while he carried it across the room. Un-

fortunately the study was small and the show regretta-
bly short. Rachel let out a breath she'd been unaware of
holding as Daniel set the box down.

Daniel gave her a curious look and Rachel remembered he'd asked her a question. "Not off-limits, just—
over, I guess. My son, Mark, is a freshman at IU—Indiana University—this year and he seems to have been
the glue that held the marriage together. Without
Mark—" She shrugged.

"You don't look old enough to have a college-age
son," Daniel said, staring at her. She really didn't. Her
skin was cream-colored and smooth, her hair still vi-
brantly brown.

"Yes, well I am. I do."

"What were you, a child bride? How old are you,
anyway?" he asked, tact forgotten in his surprise.

Rachel winced. Oh well, if he hadn't realized how
close to being over the hill she was before, here came the
grand revelation. "I'm thirty-seven."

"Wow, think of it. You're only five years older than
I am and you've got a kid old enough for college while I
sit here with an eighteen-month-old. That's amazing."

"You're thirty-two?"

"Yeah, why?"

"Oh, no reason." Only five years difference. Not so
much. What was she saying? They were worlds apart.
Worlds. "And you've never been married?" How was
that possible?

"Like I said, I was working my way up to it, but the
lady in question backed out when she found out I wasn't
interested in climbing the corporate ladder. Can you put
some of my stuff on the shelves now that they're cleared
while I unpack the printer and hook it up?"

"What? Oh, sure. No problem. I wouldn't worry about your fiancée bailing out on you. Look on it as a lucky escape. The right woman will come along for you, you'll see." God, she hated saying that. It actually physically hurt to say it. Why, she couldn't imagine.

Daniel looked up from the molded foam form he was struggling to remove from the carton he'd just opened. He snorted. "Why do I doubt that? Not only do I no longer believe in something so ephemeral as *true love,* but even if it did exist, can you honestly see some woman with a grain of intelligence—and I refuse to marry a stupid one—willingly taking on everything that currently goes along with me?"

He forced the foam out of the box and far more gently began to ease his new printer up and out. "I'm not saying Todd's a lemon or anything like that, but circumstances being what they are, it would take somebody pretty special to try to make lemonade out of my life just now. Maybe I could interest Mother Teresa, what do you think?"

"She's too old for you," Rachel said, dismissing the modern day saint and happy to do it. If she couldn't have him, neither could Mother Teresa. "Besides, she's a nun. I bet she took a vow of chastity."

Daniel grunted. "Oh well, then forget it. If I'm going to be somebody's meal ticket, I'd want to get something out of the deal. I don't suppose you have any masochistic tendencies yourself?" he asked before he even realized what was going to come out of his mouth. He froze, unable to believe he'd asked something so stupid. What if she took him up on it? He could get burnt all over again.

Rachel, however, knew he was kidding. He had to be, didn't he? So she treated the question lightly. "Masochism? No, I'm out of that phase myself. I've decided to go for narcissism, personally."

Daniel shrugged, more disappointed with her flip reply than he wanted to admit. "Oh well, there you have it, then. I'm doomed to bachelorhood what with you and Mother Teresa both tied up. Listen, your hand is smaller than mine. Can you reach down underneath there and plug this in for me?"

"What? Oh, sure."

Rachel leaned over and twisted to get under the desk. Daniel almost swallowed his tongue at the view of her backside she presented. He clenched his fists in order to dispel the wave of feeling that shot through him.

"I've almost got—there."

Rachel wriggled back out and Daniel quickly raised his eyes before she could turn around and face him again. He reached for the remaining connecting cords.

"Listen, Daniel, I really think—" Rachel made a conscious effort to stop herself. While she didn't actually bite her tongue, it was a close call. She hated him sounding so, what? Desperate? Hopeless? He'd meet the right woman, it was just a matter of time. She wanted to advise him further, but knew he wouldn't appreciate it.

"Got a bottle of spray cleaner and a cloth?" Rachel asked. "I want to wipe off the shelves before I put your manuals and things up there. They're dusty."

Daniel was knee-deep in cables. He fought valiantly to stretch them from monitor to CPU, then snake the recalcitrant devils to the keyboard and back before going on to the printer. "Over there someplace," he muttered and gestured with his head as both hands were full. "I know this hooks in here somehow so why isn't it cooperating with me? And where the heck is the surge protector strip I bought?"

Rachel watched the muscles in his back bunch and stretch under the faded pocket T-shirt he wore and turned unhappily to spritz the shelves. *Once a mother, always a mother,* she thought with a sigh. For years and years, Rachel's main human contact had been with children. The level of conversation did not improve with the onset of adolescence. *Wear your safety belt. Don't speed. Be careful with that. If you drop it, it'll break. Put your dishes in the sink. Take your muddy shoes off at the door, I just washed the floor.*

The directives had become a habit and she'd found herself talking to Ron that way on occasion. *It's raining. Don't forget your rubbers and an umbrella.* Ron had not appreciated it. Rachel doubted Daniel would, either. Heck, Mark at eighteen no longer put up with it.

She was a mother hen without any chicks to follow her lead. One of her vows upon the breakup of her marriage was to elevate the level of her conversation and Rachel was determined to do it. "But it's hard when they're so darned determined to be stubborn and stupid," she said under her breath as she shoved books onto Daniel's shelves. "All he has to do is open up his eyes and see. Good grief, if I hadn't known he was kidding, I'd have seriously considered taking up his offer, and the last thing I want to do is remarry." She continued to mumble. "Well, I'm certainly not going to advise him on all the available ways to meet women. It's none of my business. I won't say a word. I won't, I won't, I won't." Rachel would not even consider that she might have less than altruistic motives for her refusal to stick her nose in his business. It wouldn't matter at all to her if this man she barely knew married.

She was talking to herself.

Daniel was momentarily distracted from his battle with the man-eating cables by the sight of Rachel arguing with herself while she unpacked his office materials. God, she was cute. Daniel couldn't help but wonder who was winning the verbal contest, Rachel 1 or Rachel 2, but having had a sister, he was just bright enough not to ask. Women could be difficult when confronted with their own peccadilloes. They delighted, however, in pointing out a man's.

Rachel knelt up straight, clasped her hands behind her back and stretched her spine in an attempt to straighten it out. Her bent-over position must have given her a kink in her back, Daniel realized and he pressed his fingers over his eyes in an attempt to keep them in their sockets as her breasts popped out beautifully from the backward stretching action. Maybe he could offer to rub her back for her.

But they were in what passed for his office. Too unprofessional, he guessed, and sighed. Theirs was, at least at this point in time, a working relationship, more's the pity.

Rachel heard Daniel's sigh. "What's the matter?" she asked and looked back over her shoulder at him.

And there, Daniel realized as he reminded himself to keep his tongue in his mouth, was a pose worthy of a pinup calendar.

"Something not going right?"

Daniel forced himself to turn back to project. He flicked on the monitor and the CPU and prepared to install the printer. "Uh, no, everything's fine. I should have this up and running in no time."

"Oh, well, good."

Yeah, good, fine, whatever. His brain was mush and he struggled to insert the programming disk that had come with the printer. Finally he succeeded and the machine hummed as the information was installed on the hard drive. "So, you, um, told me what you've been doing, but not where you're headed. What kind of job are you looking for?"

"An office job," Rachel replied promptly.

"What kind of office?"

Rachel hadn't thought that far ahead. "It doesn't matter," she finally decided. "Any kind of office."

Daniel watched information flit across his screen and punched the appropriate keys when so instructed. "Doing what?"

"Whatever they want me to do."

Daniel's eyes narrowed as things started getting a little dicey on his screen. "That's certainly specific enough."

"If you don't understand yet, you will in a few more weeks," she informed him wisely, "given your present circumstances."

Daniel snorted. "What's that supposed to mean?"

"It means an office job has a beginning time and an ending time. You punch in at nine, out at five. Ron used to come home from work and complain about what a tough eight hours it had been. It was his excuse for not helping around the house, but I'd been up at six with Mark and was still doing laundry, cleaning and a myriad other things that made the house run smoothly for him and Mark at ten o'clock that night. There's no such thing as regular working hours for a mother."

"I see what you mean," Daniel said, and was afraid that he did. He and Rachel were not that different in age, but a world apart at where they were in life. His chances of talking her into helping him out on a permanent basis were slim.

"I'm going to find a computer class somewhere because I don't understand those machines well. I think that will make me more employable."

"Good idea." And it was. Too bad. He glanced at the screen before him. The computer swore the printer was installed and ready to go. Daniel ran a test. Nothing. "Well, damn."

Rachel came and looked over his shoulder. "What's the matter?"

Daniel raked his hand through his hair and tried to ignore her proximity and the faint smell of her perfume. "It's not printing."

"Why not?"

"I don't know."

"Where's the manual?"

"Right here."

Silently, they poured over it.

"Did you do this step right here?"

"Yeah."

"What about this?"

"I think so."

An hour went by. Daniel clicked in and out of various files, trying various commands and changing settings. Rachel stayed right there with him. She was tenacious, he'd give her that.

"It's got something to do with this toolbox file thing, I just know it."

Daniel had been reduced to grunting at that point, but he clicked on that icon and fiddled with a few things in the file. "Let's try it now." The printer hummed and went into action, spitting out a beautifully printed sheet of paper that said, "Hello, my name is Daniel."

"Eureka!" Rachel screeched and squeezed his shoulders.

"Yes!" Daniel cried. "We did it!" He jumped up out of his chair and spun around to hug her. The printer was working and Rachel's beautiful breasts were pressed against his chest. What more could a man want? He kissed her in celebration of such a wonderful world.

It was meant to be a brief, impersonal salute to success against adversity, but it did not stay passionless long. It escalated and their lips stayed sealed until they were both breathless.

"My goodness," Rachel said when they finally broke apart.

Like Mae West, Daniel doubted goodness had anything to do with it, but he was too befuddled to argue the point. He stood there, breathing heavily for a moment or two while he struggled to marshall his thoughts together, any thoughts. "I didn't mean to do that," he said. "You kiss great and I can't say I'm sorry, but I didn't mean to do it."

"I understand," Rachel said quickly. "Really. I've, um, got to go now. Yes, I've got to go."

Daniel forced his arms to stay at his sides and not grab her again. He'd already pressed his luck. He just hoped the price wasn't more than he wanted to pay. "Will you come back? Tomorrow or the next day? I'll pay you. Think of it as a nontraditional office job. You can set your own hours," he offered temptingly.

"Not tomorrow," she quickly decided. Rachel needed time to think. "Maybe the next day, all right?" Then she felt bad for not helping out more, when he so obviously needed it. "For a whole day, all right? I'll watch Todd in the morning, then help you when he's down for his nap."

"That'd be terrific," he agreed quickly, not giving her time to change her mind. "And I'll get an ad in the paper tomorrow or the next day. This will be short-term, you'll see."

"Okay," Rachel said as she backed out of the study. Her voice still sounded breathy and she just couldn't believe she'd kissed a man on such short acquaintance. "Day after tomorrow."

"Right." He nodded seriously and watched her flee.

Chapter Four

Todd rejoined the land of the living within twenty minutes of Rachel's leaving. Daniel managed another hour of work by bringing into the study a box of toys, several small boxes of raisins and a bag of pretzel rods. Todd ground raisins into the carpet with his fingertips and banged on the furniture with the pretzel rods, loosening their salt and leaving it sprinkled everywhere. Daniel ignored it all because he was actually getting some things accomplished. He'd vacuum later, after Todd was back in bed for the night, he decided.

Around five o'clock Daniel stretched and decided to pack it in. He picked up Todd and hugged him, getting the mushy end of a pretzel rod in his neck by way of thanks. "You're a good sport, kiddo," he said as Todd rode his hip down the hall to the kitchen. "You played by yourself for quite a while there. Now you get your reward." Daniel set the toddler down on the fake pebble linoleum flooring, ceremoniously unlatched the child locks and opened two of the lower cabinet doors in front of Todd. "There you go, sport. Help yourself."

As Todd eagerly leaned forward, intent· on getting his hands on all those shiny pots and pans, Daniel went to investigate the contents of the refrigerator. "At least I know enough now to realize mealtimes are inviolable. You've been a whole lot happier since Rachel told me to treat those three time slots as though they'd been handed down from the Mount as the eleventh commandment. *Thou shalt not be late with Todd's dinner. His lunch or breakfast, either,*" Daniel intoned and laughed as he pulled open the produce drawer and removed a bag of salad makings.

"Too bad Rachel's so burnt out from that marriage of hers." Daniel thought about the kiss they'd shared. It *really* was too bad. "She'd only be perfect to help me out here." Objectively speaking, it wasn't a bad idea, especially with her being so easy on the eyes and well, she was just nice to be around. Not that he was looking for anything more than a nanny. Daniel snapped his fingers. "I wonder if it's too late to call that ad in." Probably. Oh well. "Tomorrow."

Rachel was coming back on Friday, the day after tomorrow. Maybe he'd work on her some more then, only he'd have to be a lot smoother. He picked a pot up off the floor, filled it with water and set it on the rangetop to boil.

He had to stop daydreaming about Rachel or he'd be in too deep. Daniel watched the bubbles start to form in the pot. Marie had made him realize what a crock love was. He'd become determined after that fiasco to use more of an intellectual approach to the personal side of his life. Logic and reason. It should work. He'd certainly had success that way in his business dealings.

So fine. He'd do that—and, objectively speaking, convincing Rachel to be his housekeeper, nanny, whatever you wanted to call it, was a brilliant plan. Rachel had a lot of pluses on her side. Daniel started to enumerate them, just as he would for any business decision.

Agewise, she was mature enough to be settled. Stability was important for a kid and he had a second sense that Rachel would be dependable.

Personalitywise, she was kind, but also down-to-earth—an important combination with a toddler. And Todd had been comfortable with her right off the bat. What did that make her? Homey? Daniel didn't think so. Her body was too lethal for homey, although Todd was undoubtedly too young to appreciate that aspect.

Daniel thought some more.

Maternal—don't forget maternal. That was important and Rachel had that going for her.

And bodywise, well, just because he didn't want to waste a lot of time searching for some kind of ephemeral *true love* garbage that probably only existed in fairy tales didn't mean Daniel had lost interest in the sexual side of life.

Rachel had a body that he'd happily follow to bed at night. Of course, it was way too soon to be thinking about anything like that, damn it anyway. Rachel was too leery of him already. He could imagine what she'd think if she knew he had designs on her body.

But it sure would be nice to have Rachel waiting in his bed when he climbed under the covers at night. Especially considering the way she kissed. Man, the woman knew how to operate a pair of lips, for sure. His groin began to ache just thinking about the brief kiss they'd shared. "And that was nothing," he assured himself. "I hate to think what would happen if I ever really got her in a clinch.'' He pictured smoke coming out of his ears followed by self-immolation.

But first he had to get her to agree to work for him. ''Come Friday I will be subtlety itself,'' he vowed as he read the back of the macaroni box. ''Smoothness personified. The lady won't know what hit her.'' But it was going to take time, he realized and sighed. And in the meantime—Daniel looked down to the child industriously emptying pans and kettles out of the cabinet by his feet. Well, he and Todd would simply muddle through. ''In the long run, though, Todd,'' he vowed, ''no matter what, things will get back to at least quasi-normalcy around here. I promise you that.''

Todd smiled happily up at him, banged a kettle lid on the floor and said, ''Cookoo. Cookoo.''

Daniel grinned back, inordinately pleased with himself that he actually understood what the toddler was after. ''Cookies, huh? Why the heck not? Cookies it is.'' He stepped over a Dutch oven and reached up into a cabinet. ''Here we go, graham crackers all around. And, hey, let's really get wild and crazy and have a glass of milk with them, what do you say?''

Todd stood and trotted over to his high chair where he waited expectantly, arms lifted. ''Cookoo. Juice. Cookoo. Juice.''

''Not exactly a sparkling conversationalist, are you, Todd?'' Daniel asked as he pulled the tray out for the boy and helped him into the chair. ''But not to worry. I'm going to try to get Rachel to help me fix that for you. I think Rachel could probably fix a lot of things around here.'' He handed Todd half of a graham cracker and again remembered how Rachel had made a point of using a lot of descriptive words when talking to Todd.

"Here's your cookie, Todd. Look, it's brown and it's a square. See? Four right angles and all sides equal—a square."

Todd took the cracker and mashed it against the high chair tray. Several small chunks broke off, which, one by one, he grasped carefully between thumb and forefinger and conveyed to his mouth before using a wet fingertip to stab at the crumbs, then sucking the bits off his fingertips as well.

"Yes, well now it's a triangle—sort of, although there's this little bit left on this side. Not really a trapezoid, though. Tell you what, we'll call it an extremely lopsided quadrilateral and let it go at that."

Daniel used Rachel's technique of only putting a small amount of liquid into the cup and refilling it if need be. He'd realized right away that her system allowed for much smaller wipe-ups when Todd dumped his cup—which Todd did on a regular basis. He set the tumbler with half an inch of milk in the bottom on the high chair tray. "And look at this, kiddo, for your dining pleasure this afternoon, we've got a yellow cup. Nothing cheesy about this restaurant, hey, Todd? We've got cups in every color of the rainbow. Why don't you chug some of this good white milk down? It's good for your bones— lots of calcium. Yum."

Todd floated what remained of his graham cracker in his milk and waited until the cracker was good and soggy before he fished it out. It squished nicely through his fingers and he rubbed it on his face and in his freshly shampooed hair while Daniel's back was turned. He took a swig of his milk, then poured the rest onto his high chair tray and played in the puddle.

By the time Daniel had drained the macaroni, added the cheese, stirred in a can of tuna and turned around,

Todd had created a real mess. Daniel sighed and wondered if getting things back on a normal footing would actually help in this situation. Todd would still be a toddler, after all. It would probably be years before he was civilized enough to take out in company. "I'm doomed," he announced to his nephew. "If I can't bring Rachel around, I might as well forget female companionship for the next fifteen to twenty years, that's all, just write it off."

Todd laughed merrily and Daniel gave up. Why waste a plate on this little cannibal? He spooned the macaroni mixture right onto the tray and poured a puddle of apple sauce next to it.

"There you go, Todd. Gourmet dining. Go to it." And when Todd did just that, Daniel shuddered. "Holy mackerel. You're going to have to clean up your act sometime over the next eighteen years, kid. You're not fit for civilized company and no girl in her right mind is going to want to go out with you—not once she's seen you eating." Daniel had to turn away from the sight before him.

Of course, thinking of Todd's prospective dates brought to mind girls, which brought up women, and then, what else? He was back to Rachel, of course. "I've got to stop doing this." He groaned. "Before I'm in real danger of losing my mind."

Daniel gave brief thought to getting a little more work done after dinner, but it became rapidly apparent he'd used up all Todd's goodwill. Todd would not be put down. He pointed and whined and when Daniel handed him whatever it was he'd wanted, Todd would throw it down and cry.

It wasn't as if the child was open to reason, either. Daniel tried briefly and reason was not Todd's strong suit.

"So now what am I supposed to do?" Daniel asked nobody in particular. Where was Rachel when he needed her? Sitting in her apartment with pillows behind her back and her feet up, sipping wine coolers, that's where. She'd probably put a damn time clock in her new kitchen, Daniel thought rather nastily. Punched out on it every day at five on her way to the living-room sofa and the damn wine coolers.

Daniel raked his free hand through his hair as Todd tossed away the stacking doughnut toy he'd just demanded and been given. The child stuck out his lip so petulantly that Daniel almost groaned.

"Distraction," Daniel muttered to himself. "That's what we need. A distraction."

Daniel lugged Todd, who'd grown heavier with every passing minute of the past hour, back to the nursery. With one hand he grabbed the satin-bound blanket from the crib, then sat in the rocking chair. Arranging the blanket as Rachel had, so that the binding touched Todd's cheek, neck and hand, he held the child against his chest and began to rock.

"Like a miracle." Daniel sighed with relief.

Within moments, Todd found his thumb and measurably calmed down. Daniel continued to rock, determined to enjoy what was sure to be a brief period of peace and quiet while Todd was awake.

"Only one more hour until bedtime," he reassured himself. "You can make it that long. Just sixty more minutes." But it would be a lot easier if somebody lived in with them full-time. One of them could be doing the dinner dishes and vacuuming the raisins and pretzel salt out of the study carpet while the other did this. Instead Daniel still had to look forward to all of that once Todd was down. He'd be up until midnight and Todd would be ready to face the new day by six-thirty tomorrow morning—at the latest. Oh, God. How did single parents do it? And how had it all come down on his own head without even the pleasure of the conception? Life could be damned unfair at times, that was all there was to it. Damned unfair.

Daniel's mind wandered. He stroked Todd's head and the boy snuggled closer. It was a trick he'd learned by observing Rachel.

And there he was, back to *her* again.

Ah, Rachel—now there was a woman and a half. Besides all her personality attributes, Rachel was what, aesthetically pleasing? Well she was, but—Daniel settled for easy on the eyes. Extremely, unbelievably easy on the eyes, especially for someone with a kid old enough to be in college. Why Rachel was so incredibly easy on the eyes, Daniel's jeans were becoming darned uncomfortable as he thought about the way she looked and the way she moved. My, oh my.

Daniel rocked harder as thoughts of Rachel's well-formed body raced through his mind. No one would ever accuse her of being anorexic, no indeed, but the padding fell in all the right places as far as Daniel was concerned. His view of the proper proportions for the female body had changed abruptly with his unwitting assumption of fatherhood.

Of what good were thin, bony shoulders to a tired child needing to rest his head? None. None at all. And Rachel, he couldn't help but notice, along with her other attributes also came equipped with full soft-looking breasts made for pillowing Todd's head when she rocked him. Daniel rather ached to rest his own head against her softness, truth be told. "Too soon." He sighed. "Much too soon." What a pity. "A damn shame." He'd scare her off for sure and be left with nothing but his fantasies—good though they were, they would not keep him warm on a winter's cold night and definitely would be insufficient to hold him over the long haul of Todd's childhood and adolescence.

"And I'm afraid I am indeed in for the long haul before I'll be fit for dating again. And by then I'll be too old to care." Daniel sighed yet again.

After a seemingly interminable evening during which Daniel had the songs to *The Little Mermaid* and *Beauty and the Beast* all but memorized, Todd finally conked out.

It was eight-thirty, but felt more like midnight. He wanted nothing more than to fall into bed himself and sleep the sleep of the righteous.

Instead he pulled the vacuum cleaner out of the back hall closet and went to vacuum the rug. Rachel would be there to help again on Friday. All he had to do was get through Thursday.

It was sure to be the longest day of his life.

And it was. The day kick-started with Cheerios smushed into banana pieces and another dumped cup of milk. Then, after breakfast there were several other times when Daniel noticed that the sun seemed stuck, or at the very least stalled in its trajectory, but the day did ever so gradually wind down, much to his gratitude. By the time Todd let him know he was awake from his nap, Daniel had even accomplished a few things in his office—that was minus the time he'd spent peeling the two raisins he'd missed vacuuming the night before off the bottom of his bare foot, of course.

Still, by then it was almost four o'clock of another day almost successfully muddled through and surely that was reason for a small celebration? "Hey, Todd, you want to go for a walk? Let's get your stroller out. We can go up to the store and pick out something special for dinner." And when they walked up the street, Rachel might be out in front of her building, you never knew.

Todd climbed willingly into his stroller and Daniel ambled up the street, but no Rachel. He kept his head straight so as not to appear too obvious in case she was there, but he searched the park out of the corners of his eyes as they went by.

Nothing.

Dejected and angry with himself for feeling that way, he continued another block and a half to the grocery store. "How about some soup?" he asked Todd as he lifted a couple of cans of the heat-and-serve variety off the shelf and displayed them to the toddler. "Chicken vegetable or split pea, what do you think, champ?"

"If he picks the split pea, I'll work for free tomorrow."

Daniel spun around and faced the voice that had come from behind him. "Rachel! Hi! What are you doing here?" Stupid question. It was a grocery store. Might she be shopping for food? "Um, what's wrong with split pea soup?" Not much better. Surely he could come up with a better conversational gambit than that.

But Rachel didn't seem to mind. She ruffled Todd's hair and responded, "Nothing, if you don't mind wearing it."

Daniel looked at the feminine hand resting on his nephew's head and wished he could reach out and touch her as easily as she did Todd. "Excuse me?"

Rachel smiled down at Todd, then up at Daniel. "I think it's an acquired taste that has to develop over the years. No self-respecting toddler I've ever met would swallow that swill. Five will get you ten if you try to feed him split pea soup for dinner he'll just spray it all over you."

Daniel's eyes widened at the mental image she'd created. He looked down at his white knit shirt and khaki cotton shorts. He put the can back on the shelf, not bothering to restrain a shudder. "No, thanks."

Rachel laughed. "Think about it. I bet you didn't like it as a kid, either. I was in my teens before I'd eat split pea. I'm still waiting for Mark to develop a taste for it."

He didn't argue. "I think we'll go for the chicken vegetable."

"Wise man." Rachel grinned at Todd and couldn't help but reach for him. She swung him up and out of the stroller, cocked one hip out and bounced Todd on it while she talked to him. "So what do you think, kiddo? Are you going to be good for me tomorrow? I just saved your life here, you know."

Todd giggled at whatever the joke was and grabbed for her dangly earrings. "Pretty."

Rachel tilted her head back and out of harm's way. "Oh, no, you don't, you little terror. I've got your number now. No way are you going to pull my earrings out the hard way, no sir."

Daniel watched the byplay between Rachel and his nephew. Would he ever be that natural with Todd? And it was silly to feel left out. But he did.

He stood there, feeling stupid and inept. Then he began to examine Rachel as she continued to talk silly talk to Todd. She had a slender waist and hips that flared out just the right amount for Todd to straddle, Daniel noticed. For the first time he could remember, Daniel appreciated how God had excelled in combining form and function with his design for the female body. It appealed to the adult and worked for the child. That God, what a guy. Probably could have taken first prize in an architectural contest—if He'd needed the ego boost and bothered to enter one—with that particular design.

"Excuse me."

Daniel glanced over to the source of the impatient sounding interruption and realized he had the aisle all but blocked. "Sorry," he apologized and edged Todd's stroller out of the way. The woman sailed through without another word. He had no idea how long she'd been waiting for them to notice her. He'd only had eyes for Rachel.

Once again, she was wearing walking shorts. She probably did that on purpose—a safety precaution kind of thing. Who knew what would happen to the blood pressure of any men who might innocently venture out of doors when Rachel passed by if she showed more leg in public? If her thighs were half as well turned as her calves, well—

Daniel probably would have done something stupid—like drooled right around then, but Rachel returned Todd to his stroller and playtime seemed to be over. They walked companionably to the end of the aisle. Getting one foot successfully down in front of the other gave him something to concentrate on other than Rachel's legs and Daniel concentrated on it for all he was worth.

As it was, he was barely able to maintain what was left of his dignity. As he followed her to the end of the aisle, he reminded himself that autumn was just around the corner. Rachel would be switching to slacks before he knew it. Hopefully then Daniel wouldn't have to try so hard not to stare at those glorious appendages, but he knew it would be touch and go—provided she was still around. She had to be. God, please let her be.

"Oh, God," he said under his breath and this time it was definitely a prayer. "Let her see how sensible this would all be. She could stop her job search right here and now. It's a made-in-heaven opportunity for both of us. She could move in, save herself apartment rent, then I could—we could—" He cleared his throat. "So, Rachel, how's the unpacking going?"

She turned back and almost knocked his thongs off with her smile. Her husband must have been a real cretin to let this woman get away.

"Well, thanks."

"Good, good. Get a lot accomplished today?"

"Yes. I've only got a few boxes left to unpack, as a matter of fact."

"That's nice." Play your cards right here, he cautioned himself. You've got to draw her in carefully. Get her in the net without her hearing the swish of it coming down on her and flitting off. "Well, so long as you've gotten so much accomplished, maybe you've got a little more time now? Maybe I could talk you into coming a little earlier, say in time for breakfast and staying a bit later? Eat dinner with us? Might as well eat together. If we work together, making a meal would only take half as long. We've both got to eat, right? No point in duplicating the effort. Provided there's nothing else you need to do right then, of course." Would she go for it? he wondered. It had all certainly sounded reasonable enough to him. That's if he didn't stop to think about why sharing breakfast and dinner with Rachel *really* appealed to him.

By then they were standing in the checkout line. Rachel caught the slight strain in his voice and wondered what it was about. She studied Daniel carefully while she waited to pay for her box of oatmeal and packaged chicken breast.

He was still disturbingly handsome; she'd probably never be comfortable with what Daniel Van Scott did to her pulse and libido, but the poor man obviously needed some help. There was a jelly stain on his collar that he probably wasn't even aware of. It spoke of peanut-butter-and-jelly sandwiches for lunch and sticky little fingers wrapped around Daniel's neck before he'd had a chance to wipe them off. ''Did you call in the ad, Daniel?''

He snapped his fingers. "Shoot, no, I forgot again." He made a production of checking his wrist. "It's too late now. I'll have to try to remember to do it tomorrow."

"Daniel, that's something you really need to take care of. You simply can't do this all by yourself."

"You're right. I know." And he did. Maybe he was a fool, but he still had his hopes pinned on his own agenda. "I'll take care of it, I promise, but about tomorrow...?"

"Cash, check or charge?"

Rachel turned her attention briefly to the cashier. "Cash," she responded and put the dividing stick between her two items and Daniel's can of soup. It seemed sort of symbolic, but not worth much in terms of real self-protection. She was a sap and absolutely no good at putting her own needs first, not even now when she'd learned the hard way how little her efforts were appreciated once the need was gone. Still, there was something so pathetic about that lone can of soup—

"Tell you what, Daniel, tomorrow being Friday, maybe I could come early and at least help with breakfast. I'll still have the weekend to get everything I want done taken care of."

Daniel was elated. It wasn't everything, but it was a start. And he was not about to look a gift horse in the mouth. Besides, he'd have all day to work on her for dinner. "That'd be terrific, Rachel. You have no idea how much I appreciate this."

"That'll be two dollars and sixty-nine cents, please. Paper or plastic?"

"Wait for us," he urged when she paid her bill and received her sack. "We'll walk you home." Daniel was euphoric on the way back down the street. He'd made it through Thursday. Friday was practically here and that meant an entire day to work on her. *To be with her.* He dismissed the thought. He had to think of his objective—child care for Todd. Surely between Todd and himself one of them would be able to get some kind of hook into Rachel. They dropped Rachel off in front of her two-flat. "See you in the morning."

She waved and agreed. "Yes, I'll be there bright and early."

Daniel managed to wait to pump his fist and yell, "Yes," until she was inside her door, but it was a close thing. He took Todd home and fed him the soup and some canned fruit cocktail for dinner. They stacked blocks for a while, then he took Todd into the nursery and tried to rock him. He'd read an article that it was important to have a bedtime ritual and a quiet-time just before lights-out and Daniel was determined to do the right things for Todd.

Todd, however, seemed to have his own ideas.

"Todd get down," he stated emphatically and scrambled off Daniel's lap. "Book." Todd went to the shelving unit along one wall, retrieved a picture book and returned to Daniel. He lifted his arms. "Up me," he said.

Daniel lifted him back onto his lap and opened the cardboard book to the first page. "What's this, Todd?" he asked.

"Kitty. *Meow, meow.*"

"Good job." Daniel pointed to the adjacent page. "And this?" Frankly he didn't see why anyone would divorce a woman like Rachel regardless of *how* they'd come to gain her hand—and since she was so young to have a kid in college, he had his suspicions about that. Well, whatever mistakes she'd made, she'd paid for them. She was free to do what she wanted now. He only hoped that what she wanted was him—and Todd.

"Doggie."

"And what does the dog say?" Mentally Daniel geared himself for the morning. He suspected from some of Rachel's remarks she'd married once for the sake of a child. That could work both for and against him. No doubt she liked children and Todd was definitely a child, but she probably felt used. He'd be walking a fine line on this one, but by God, he was more convinced than ever that the prize would be worth the effort.

"Doggie goes *woof!*"

"You're *woof* right again, old buddy." Cautiously optimistic now, he smiled down at his nephew. "Todd, you must be the smartest almost two-year-old I've ever seen." And right then, at that moment, he was as sure of Todd's brilliance as he was that Rachel's eyes were brown.

Rachel was coming tomorrow. Already Daniel could feel an easing of the tension in his neck—the tension that had been a constant companion since he'd taken custody of Todd. Heck, by tomorrow afternoon, he might actually have things enough under control to make a few phone calls in an effort to start recruiting some clients.

That would be good, but you know what would be better? he asked himself. Kicking back and just being with Rachel and Todd. Maybe the three of them could go to the park or, even better, he could wait until Todd's naptime, then spend some time getting to know Rachel. Yeah, just the two of them, that was the ticket.

When he realized the direction his thoughts were taking, Daniel started, which in turn caused Todd to jump. Daniel soothed him while castigating himself. What in the world was wrong with him? Getting his business profitable had to be his top concern and he'd darn well better keep that important priority firmly in mind.

Chapter Five

Rachel locked the door to her apartment at 7:44 the next morning and pressed Daniel's bell promptly at a quarter to eight. She smoothed her hair back into place, checked to make sure her shirt was tucked neatly into her waistband and wondered why she was so nervous about seeing Daniel again. "Hi," she said when he answered her ring. He was just a man. Just a man. Just a—

"Hi, yourself," Daniel responded and swung the screen door open for her. She looked good again this morning, he decided, and was no longer surprised. The morning breeze played with her hair while her smile played havoc with his heart rate. Thank God he didn't have to pass a physical anytime soon.

She held out an apple to him. It sported a dark bruise on one side. "I think this is yours," Rachel told him. "I found it under a bush when I came out this morning. I don't know how I managed to miss it before now."

He took the apple and studied it, not quite sure what to do with it. "Oh well—thanks."

Rachel smiled sunnily in response and Daniel knew that if the apple was too mushy to eat, he wouldn't be able to throw it away in front of her. Instead he'd probably have it bronzed or something. Anything so she'd think her thoughtfulness—however misplaced—was appreciated. Which it was, of course, just not nearly so much as the gift of her presence.

"You're welcome," she said to him with that same heart-stopping smile that actually had him laying a hand on his chest over his heart to check that it still beat. *Yes, there it went, thank God.* When he looked back to Rachel, she hadn't moved but was still standing out on the porch, looking expectantly up at him.

Daniel started. "Oh! Come on in, but watch your step," he warned as he leaned forward to hold the door, embarrassed at being caught gawking at her as if he were an adolescent with his first crush.

He glanced down to make sure she didn't stumble on the lone step up. *Damn,* he thought. *She even has beautiful feet.* He'd never been struck dumb by a pair of feet, not once in all his dating years. He'd been around Todd too long, that had to be it. His brain had gone dysfunctional from the lack of stimulation required by anything over an eighteen-month-old's level.

Even her toes were cute, with their nails left unvarnished and plain. But then, they didn't need color or polish to turn him on. What was it his mother used to say? Something about not gilding a lily? Oh, man, just look down there. Those perfect feet were complemented by a set of slim ankles that flared out into the perfectly proportioned calves he'd noticed the afternoon before. And while he'd thought yesterday's sneakers had shown her legs off nicely, Daniel was forced to admit that the slender strapped sports sandals she wore today were absolutely lethal.

Daniel had a tough time keeping his eyes off her legs as he followed her back through the house to the kitchen. Jeez Louise, had it been that long since he'd been around a female? He had to get a grip before he did something really dumb and scared the poor woman off. *You need her,* he reminded himself. *Don't do anything stupid, like jumping her bones out there on the kitchen floor. It was too hard to be comfortable and she'd be ticked, what with Todd being right there and all—and you, you dumb cluck, would be right back in the same type of situation you swore never to put yourself into again. You weren't going to get involved like that again, remember? Remember? It only leads to heartache. Remember? Get a grip, man. You need her, but not that way.*

Daniel took a deep breath to calm himself and by dint of sheer willpower, got his priorities more or less back into place—mostly less. He was afraid keeping his hands to himself was going to be an iffy proposition at best during the day. Why did he do these things to himself? he wondered. Wouldn't it be a heck of a lot easier to simply admit defeat here—after all Rachel had made it pretty clear she didn't want the job he was offering—and just place the ad in the paper and be done with it?

Maybe. Probably. He just wasn't ready to give in quite yet. Somehow his pride was now at stake. Besides, sometimes you simply had to go with your gut instincts and his gut was telling him—well, never mind, there was a toddler in the house after all.

Rachel found Todd already ensconced in his high chair. He was happily smashing banana slices into the small mound of Cheerios on the tray in front of him. She stopped just inside the doorway and smiled at the picture he made. He reminded her a lot of Mark when he'd been this age. "Hi, Todd."

He waved hands dripping with the banana goo he'd made when straining his breakfast through his fingers. "Juice! Todd wants juice!"

Rachel laughed and moved into the room. "Okay, tiger, juice coming up. You want orange juice or white juice? And what's the magic word?

"Peez!"

"That'll work." She headed to the refrigerator to get the juice, yes, but also to move away from Daniel. He disturbed her—disturbed her greatly, and she didn't like it, not one little bit. The man was entirely too male, she supposed that must be it. He was too manly at a time in her life when she wasn't too terribly enamored of even the wimpiest of the species. And none of that made the slightest bit of sense at all.

She reached into the refrigerator for the jug of orange juice, but even with her back to him, still felt Daniel's eyes on her.

It was like watching a movie starring Jimmy Stewart, Rachel decided. No matter what role he played, you never lost sight of the fact that that was Jimmy Stewart up there on the screen. That's how it was with Daniel. The clothing, the job, the setting, none of that would matter. When a woman looked at Daniel—heck, you didn't even have to be looking at him. Why, right now her back was to him and she was still totally aware of him—anyway, the first thought in a woman's head would be: *Man. Exceedingly dangerous homo sapiens manly type male.*

Well, she was here because she felt sorry for him and his situation, and that was the only reason. The rest was inconsequential. She would *make* it inconsequential. She was strong, and if necessary, she'd repeat all the reasons she was helping out here over and over again in her head until her body got the message or she was able to leave, which she would do at precisely five o'clock that afternoon, dinner sharing be damned. She'd make them a good lunch instead.

Behind her, Daniel breathed a sigh of relief. Rachel had moved in the nick of time. He wondered if she knew how tempting her backside was. He'd been so busy admiring that posterior of hers, he'd almost bumped into the door frame and missed the opening into the kitchen. Daniel passed a hand over his face. Knocking himself out in his own house was no way to correct the klutz impression he'd probably made when he'd half killed himself and Todd by tripping in her front yard.

He was cool, he reminded himself. He was suave. He also needed to get a grip—immediately.

Rachel looked over her shoulder at him when he finally followed her into the room. "Have you eaten yet, Daniel?"

"What? Oh, yes. I had some cereal with my friend here. That's my bowl over there. I'll wash it up and—"

"No, you go get started on—whatever it is you need to start on. If you're going to run a business from home, you need to get into the habit of keeping business hours right off the bat, I would think. Todd and I will be sure to stay out of your way until at least lunchtime."

She smiled at him and it was all Daniel could do to refrain from swearing. How did she *do* that to him? He didn't know one single other female of his acquaintance, Marie included, that could jack up his pulse rate as she did with nothing but a look. It was as maddening as all hell. Frustrating, too.

"I'll clean up the breakfast mess," Rachel continued, innocently unaware of the havoc she was wreaking on Daniel's insides.

Rachel continued to smile hopefully up at him while she waited for his response. *Please let him agree and just go about his business.* She wanted him out of there. Her sole purpose in coming today, she still insisted to herself, was to lend a helping hand to a guy obviously in need of one and there was no need for her peace of mind to suffer so unduly in the process.

Just look at him, she thought as she swept her eyes over his form. This morning Daniel wore jeans so snug they hugged his butt and molded themselves right to his thighs as faithfully as gelatin took on the shape of its mold, only his butt didn't jiggle when he moved. We were talking firm here, unbelievably firm—serious workout firm. Then he'd gone and topped the jeans with a blue polo-style cotton knit shirt that tried as hard as it could to stretch over his broad shoulders. It was a valiant effort, but Daniel's shoulders were so darn broad that it was a miracle he wasn't busting out of the seams. On top of everything else, the color of the shirt came darn close to matching those eyes, which had had a hypnotic effect on her from the start. Now that they were accented—well, Rachel figured she'd be in serious trouble any moment.

Daniel had also left the shirt hanging free at his waist and after dragging her eyes away from his, she now noticed how the loose fabric shamelessly tempted her to slip a hand up under the hem and personally check out for herself what appeared to be washboard abdominal muscles.

Dropping her line of vision once again, she saw he was also barefoot, which lent a kind of intimacy to the kitchen scene Rachel could do quite nicely without.

"You don't look any worse for the wear after your accident the other day," she blurted, needing to say something to fill the absence of sound in the room.

Daniel shrugged. "Just a couple of scratches. I'll live."

Rachel grabbed the sponge and began swabbing the countertop. He'd cleaned up well. Real well. "Your knees are all right?" she asked and knew she shouldn't have as her eyes dropped once more to the legs faithfully outlined through his denim jeans. Oh, God, what a bod. She refused to embarrass herself by throwing her middle-age body at such magnificence. But it was going to be tough going. Real tough. Rachel promised herself that if she made it through the day, she'd remove herself from temptation and never come back.

She almost groaned out loud at the personal cruelty of such a promise, but she simply had to do it. She refused to be part of a crowd. Look at him. He probably had a constant stream of nubile young things popping out of the woodwork, begging him to take their tax work whether April 15 was approaching or not. Here it was barely into September and Rachel had a sudden urge to look up her W-2's herself. That inexplicable itch had her deathly afraid of making a thirty-seven-year-old fool of herself.

And with the big four-oh staring her in the face in three short years, she had to remind herself that there was no fool like an old fool.

"My knees are okay, but I may have to change into shorts. The scratches are rubbing a bit."

Rachel wouldn't mind rubbing—she ground her teeth together. "Really, Daniel," she said, grabbing his cereal bowl and grasping it in a death grip. "You need to take full advantage of the time I'm here. Go into your study and close the door. Pretend you're a businessman and don't worry about anything else until I call you for lunch, okay?" *Please?* The kitchen was becoming positively claustrophobic and Rachel doubted it had anything to do with the room size. Daniel was crowding her, maybe not physically, but definitely emotionally. She barely contained a sigh of relief when Daniel made motions that indicated he was going to heed her plea.

"Well, okay, if you're sure..."

Rachel nodded. "I'm sure, now shoo." She flicked her fingers at him in a dismissing motion.

"Call me if you need me."

"I will."

Daniel pointed down the short hallway. "I'll be right in there."

Why didn't he just leave? Rachel felt like screaming. "I know. Not to worry. Say 'bye-bye' to Uncle Daniel, Todd."

Obediently Todd opened and closed his fist several times and said, "Bye-bye."

Rachel leaned against the counter and closed her eyes when Daniel finally disappeared. She'd do better as she got used to him, she told herself. She'd have to—it was either that or go on blood pressure medication. After rinsing Daniel's cereal bowl, she tucked it into the dishwasher and turned to Todd. "Okay, champ, let's clean you up, start a load of laundry and then go out into the yard. It's a beautiful day in the neighborhood." Did Mr. Rogers still say that? Was he even still on the air?

After removing the lid from the green plastic turtle shaped sandbox she found on the patio, Rachel spent some time weeding the neglected flower bed that curled around the house. While she did so, she kept an eye on Todd as he alternated between dumping sand out of the box and pushing a large metal truck around the patio and through the mess he was creating there with the sand.

Daniel sat in his study, trying to concentrate. He was disgusted and irritated with himself because he simply couldn't seem to focus on the task. Here was the golden opportunity to accomplish things while he was awake enough to know what he was doing. He'd prayed for this chance and all he had to show for it was a list of lame excuses he'd come up with to go out and join Rachel and Todd playing in the sand. Pathetic.

"What I need is a sugar jolt," he decided. "Maybe I'll go out and make some lemonade." The day was really warming up, after all, and Rachel and Todd might appreciate something to drink as well. He could just step out into the yard and see if they'd like—oh, God, there he went again. Daniel forcibly reminded himself that it wasn't good to let anybody get to him this way. It could only lead to trouble. But still, he really *really* wanted to go out and join them, and it wasn't because he wanted to build a sand castle.

Grimly Daniel opened one of the file cabinets Rachel had started on two days before and forced himself back on task. Once he finished this, he still had to call the phone company and get a business line brought in.

He had to find a decent printer and order new business cards.

He needed to get that damn ad into the paper. Um, maybe he'd leave that one for tomorrow.

Today he would figure out how the heck the internal fax on his new computer worked.

Daniel's eyes strayed to the window one last time—he swore it was the last, and—Rachel and Todd had disappeared

"Where'd they go?" Had something happened to them?

Daniel stepped over a box and moved closer to the window just in time to catch the gate slapping shut behind Rachel as she pushed Todd in his stroller out of the yard.

She must be taking him for a walk.

Daniel took a deep breath and willed his heart back down into his chest cavity. Talk about overreacting. Kids needed lots of fresh air. Walks were good for them.

So there wasn't enough fresh air right there in the backyard?

Daniel could not believe the thoughts coming out of his own head. And if *he* couldn't believe them—

And how incredibly stupid to feel deserted!

But he did.

"Well, damn," Daniel said as he checked his watch. "It's ten o'clock. I'm entitled to a break, aren't I? I'd have gone with them if she'd bothered to tell me her plans." But Rachel hadn't and suddenly taking a lemonade break lost all appeal.

"So fine," Daniel muttered. "Who needs them? Not me. I'll just stay in here and get—all kinds of things accomplished, that's what. I might even work straight through lunch. Heck, they probably wouldn't miss me if I did." He ground his teeth as he listened to the self-pitying words coming out of his mouth. He sounded like an idiot. "This is stupid," Daniel said. "Really stupid." His hands clenched in frustration and he imme-

diately loosened them again. His fingers were digging
into his palms. Daniel sighed, remembering how he'd
stumbled a bit walking home from the grocery store with
Rachel the afternoon before. He'd been watching her
hips sway and been momentarily distracted. "No wonder they didn't want me along. She probably thinks I
make a habit out of falling all over myself. She's probably afraid of the damage I'd do if I crashed on top of
her or Todd. Damn."

After that pathetic display of self-pity, Daniel managed to stay focused on his tasks long enough to make
several phone calls and begin to work on understanding
his new computer. He was deep into the owner's manual when he heard pans clattering out in the kitchen.
"They're back!" he told himself and for some reason he
preferred not delving into, his mood lifted consider-
ably.

He refused to go rushing out there, but when he returned to his work, a smile took root and erased his
frown. He found it much easier to concentrate with a
little slamming and banging going on as background
noise. It had to be Todd, Daniel thought, his lips curling further as he pictured the scene in the kitchen. Todd
would be pulling all the pots out of the lower cabinets
again.

Daniel decided to finish his current task, then go out
and help Rachel with lunch. "Okay, let's see. Type in the
command, double click here. Uh-huh, uh-huh." He
glanced back over to the manual. "Choose proper con-
figuration for your setup," he read. "All right, no
problem. I can do that."

By eleven forty-five, Daniel almost had his machine
on-line, but couldn't concentrate another moment. The
smells working their way under the study door were

more than any mere mortal man could be expected to bear. His stomach rumbled in what had to be a knee-jerk type of response and his salivary glands were engaged in a do-or-die attempt to drown his teeth.

Basically he was starved. For the moment, he'd have to settle for food. Time to go save Rachel from the little monster so that lunch could get on the table.

"I just hope whatever it is that smells so good is almost ready to eat," Daniel mumbled as he tossed the manual aside and rose from his chair. He was hoping to set the table and dig right in. "Rachel's not going to understand it if I start nibbling on her succulent little body instead of lunch." See? It was just that kind of thought slippage he was going to have to watch out for.

He reached the kitchen just as Rachel removed an obviously homemade blueberry pie from the oven. God, she could cook, too. Deep purple juice bubbled out of the pie's steam slits and it smelled better than he remembered sex feeling, although Daniel thought he ought to make allowances for how long it had been. What with everything that had been going on in his life, his memory may have dimmed. "God, Rachel, tell me you got vanilla ice cream to go along with that and I'll drag you down to the justice of the peace right this afternoon."

Rachel laughed, pretty sure he was kidding. Pretty sure. "I was going to call you in another minute or so, Daniel. Lunch is almost ready."

As if he couldn't tell. His salivary glands were in overdrive—had been for half an hour. "Sweetheart, if I could interest you in cooking like this every day, I promise you'd never once have to call me to the table. The smells alone have been driving me crazy for a good thirty minutes." A sudden movement at ground level caught his eye. "Todd, no. No climbing. The pie's hot.

It's got to cool down first. Rachel, you could have thrown together some sandwiches. I'm glad you didn't, but it wasn't my intention to wear you out.'' Especially when she was being so skittish about committing herself. He wanted to talk her into taking the job permanently and he didn't want her to find it too burdensome.

Rachel pushed hair off her damp forehead with her sleeve. ''Todd, you heard Uncle Daniel. Get down. Hot.'' Rachel turned her attention back to Daniel. ''It's slowly coming back to me. But I'd forgotten how fast they are, how quickly they can get into anything and everything,'' she confessed. She might as well admit to her failings and get it over with. Daniel would probably never want her back, which was okay because she shouldn't, uh, didn't want to come back anyway. ''He got away from me in the store and managed to give himself a bit of a split lip, I'm afraid.''

''Oh, yeah? How'd he do that?'' Daniel crouched and inspected Todd's face. His lower lip did look a bit fatter than normal, now that Daniel examined it.

''He wanted to walk, but then he wouldn't stay with me and raced out of the end of an aisle before I could get to him and ran right into a lady coming around the corner with a grocery cart. The store manager gave me some ice and he's going to be fine, but it gave me quite a scare, I have to tell you.''

''Ouch!'' Daniel winced as he pictured the scene. It was too bad Todd had taken the bump, but it secretly made him feel a bit less inferior to know that Todd was capable of giving even Rachel a run for her money. The kid had certainly proven himself consistently capable of running rings around Daniel, that was for sure.

There was nothing like an aspiring two-year-old getting the better of you to foster feelings of inadequacy,

Daniel had discovered. He remembered his bruised knees. Yes, indeed, nothing like it.

"Hold onto him a minute while I open the oven door and get the chicken out, will you? After this morning's escapade, I don't trust him not to burn himself."

Neither did Daniel. He carefully kept Todd back while Rachel removed the poultry and baked potatoes from the oven. "You went to a lot of trouble."

Rachel shrugged. She'd pull out her hair and walk around bald before she'd admit she'd done it to impress him. "I figured if I made dinner for lunch, you could do something simple for supper after I left. It'll be easier for you this way."

It also ensured they ate properly and got all their food groups without her having to harp or worry. Once a mother, always a mother, Rachel thought with disgust. "Can you pour the milk?" she asked and mentally checked off the dairy group.

He'd rather kiss her again, but Daniel knew the time was not right for that. "Sure," he said and had to content himself with pushing her bangs back for her. He'd never been a touchy kind of person until recently, since meeting Rachel actually, but there was something about Rachel that just begged a man to—well, she cried out to be touched. She had such wonderful textures, both soft and womanly. Her skin felt like—the satin binding on Todd's blanket, her hair like the plushest of Todd's stuffed toys.

Daniel cleared his throat and dropped his hand. "I'll just get the glasses down and take care of that right now."

Rachel stared after him as he turned away and wondered what had just happened. She couldn't tell much from studying his back. Had his fingers lingered when he'd brushed the hair out of her face or was she reading an intimacy into the friendly gesture that simply hadn't been intended? Daniel seemed to be exceptionally tactile and she just wasn't used to that kind of physicality, Rachel decided as she studied his body again.

Then she forced herself to concentrate on draining the peas she'd prepared and lectured her brain to pay attention before she accidentally dumped them all into the sink.

"Do you want me to help you in your office during Todd's nap?" Rachel asked as she righted the pot. "Or would you prefer me to do laundry or something?"

Daniel watched while she carefully spooned a small quantity of peas onto a plastic plate and blew on them to cool them down. He found those pursed lips fascinating. "In the office, I think," he responded, unwilling to forgo the sweet torture of having her so close. "Oh, here's the chicken I diced up for Todd. Should I put it on his tray?"

Rachel smiled, pleased that Daniel wanted her to help him. She felt more confident now than she had earlier and she was sick of her own company. She missed Mark. She missed her old neighbors. Rachel even missed Ron. Of course, the way her mind and body were behaving so perversely lately, if she got a toothache and had a dentist take care of it, she'd probably miss that, too.

But Daniel was still looking at her questioningly, his hand hovering over a tiny mountain of minutely diced chicken. "No, put it here, on top of the peas. I'll stir in the mashed potatoes as well to stick everything together. He can eat everything all together. That way the peas and chicken won't go rolling off the tray."

Well, Rachel knew best, he guessed. "All gets mixed up in your stomach anyway, my mother always used to say," Daniel allowed, although aesthetically speaking, he considered Todd's meal a visual disaster. Yuck. He kept his mouth shut, however. Daniel filled his own plate, sat down to eat and simply refused to look in Todd's direction during the meal, although he could tell by Rachel's pleased conversation with the toddler that he was scarfing the mixture right down.

"Do you want your pie now or later?" Rachel asked and it took Daniel a moment to realize she was talking to him.

"Oh, it's still pretty hot, isn't it? Maybe I'll take a break in another hour or two when Todd wakes up and have it then." That would give him an excuse to be with her again a bit after the little one's nap. Damn, but he was clever.

"All right. Let me put Todd down and clean up and I'll be in to help you."

Daniel rose and began to clear the table. "You go right ahead. I'll just scrape these and stick them into the dishwasher." But once she was out of sight, he quickly swabbed the countertops and washed the pans she'd used as well. That would get her into the study more rapidly and he could torture himself with the subtle scent of her perfume again all the quicker. Man, he was really losing it, he thought as he turned the last pot upside down on the drain board. The bad part was, Daniel didn't know if he cared or not that his mind was going. He dried his hands on a kitchen towel and went back to his office both excited and depressed, knowing Rachel would be joining him soon.

Chapter Six

"So," Daniel said when Rachel joined him in the study fifteen minutes later, "how's it going so far today? I know Todd gave you a little grief at the store, but all in all he's a pretty cute kid, don't you think?"

Rachel slanted her head and looked at Daniel. Was he simply making conversation? Maybe he needed reassurance for some reason or another. Or did he really want to talk? Over the years, Rachel had become adept at generic conversations, mostly due to her in-laws' and husband's total lack of interest in anything she had to say.

And how are you, Rachel?

Fine, Mother Bess. I'm just fine. Even if Rachel's head was threatening to split open that day with the mother of all headaches, there was little point in saying so. Mom Bess wasn't really listening and wouldn't have responded any differently anyway. She'd have said, *Good, good, that's nice, dear.* Mother Bess ran through the social niceties with her daughter-in-law as quickly as possible so she could concentrate on the important part of her visit.

And where's that handsome grandson of mine?

Back in the family room waiting for you to get here. He wouldn't want to miss out on the ten-dollar bill you always slip him when you're here, Mom. Then Mother Bess would hand Rachel her coat as though she either hadn't a clue as to what to do with a hanger herself or was accustomed to maid service all her life—which Rachel knew wasn't the case—and head down the hall.

I'll just go and say hello. What time are we expecting Ron home?

He knew you were coming, Mom, so he came home early. He's in the family room with Mark.

Then Mother Bess would beam. *He's such a wonderful son, isn't he? Well, I'll pop my head in there and see how both my men are doing.*

You do that, Mom. Rachel would hang up her mother-in-law's coat and wonder how long she'd have to be married to Ron before his mother used her name. Then she'd go out to the kitchen and prepare whatever meal was appropriate for that time of day without any help from anybody else in the house.

Well, Rachel was tired of making polite, generic conversation. So while a *Yes, he's a darling,* followed by an, *everything has gone just fine so far today,* whether it had or not would work and certainly be apropos, she decided to forgo the niceties and say what she was really thinking.

"It's been a weird morning," Rachel announced baldly.

Daniel started and stared at her. "Weird?" That wasn't what he'd wanted to hear. "How?"

Rachel shrugged and came to peer over his shoulder. At least he hadn't said, *Good, good,* and just gone on. He'd actually heard what she'd said. "Just strange, that's all. How's the computer stuff coming along? I don't know how you make head or tails out of this stuff."

"I'm setting up the parameters for the screen saver right now. What do you mean, your morning was strange?"

"I don't know, sort of a sense of déjà vu, I guess."

"Oh." That wasn't so bad. At least he didn't think it was. "Been there, done that?"

"A little more than that. I have all these golden memories of Mark at this age, but of course a mother's memory is selective. The thing is, even the small amount of time I've spent with Todd so far brings everything— the good and the bad—all back."

Maybe this wasn't so good, Daniel thought. "What are you trying to say, Rachel?"

Rachel rested her hands on his shoulders and looked at the computer screen. "That's neat. I like all the colors. What's it for?"

Daniel, unbelievably aware of the light pressure on his shoulders, ordered his body to stay still. Men, *real* men didn't squirm under a woman's touch. "It's a screen saver. If you leave the computer on too long without using it, whatever's on the screen will eventually burn its image onto the screen. This comes on after two minutes of nonuse and keeps that from happening."

"Oh. Interesting."

"Yeah, now about this déjà vu thing..."

"It's not that big of a deal, Daniel. It was just that while Todd is cute as all get-out and I enjoyed all his antics this morning, the day-in-day-out reality of watch-

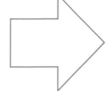

NO COST! NO OBLIGATION TO BUY!
NO PURCHASE NECESSARY!

PLAY "LUCKY 7"
AND GET FIVE FREE GIFTS!

HOW TO PLAY:

1. With a coin, carefully scratch off the silver box at the right. Then check the claim chart to see what we have for you—FREE BOOKS and a gift—ALL YOURS! ALL FREE!

2. Send back this card and you'll receive brand-new Silhouette Romance™ novels. These books have a cover price of $3.25 each, but they are yours to keep absolutely free.

3. There's no catch. You're under no obligation to buy anything. We charge nothing—ZERO—for your first shipment. And you don't have to make any minimum number of purchases—not even one!

4. The fact is thousands of readers enjoy receiving books by mail from the Silhouette Reader Service™ months before they're available in stores. They like the convenience of home delivery and they love our discount prices!

5. We hope that after receiving your free books you'll want to remain a subscriber. But the choice is yours—to continue or cancel, anytime at all! So why not take us up on our invitation, with no risk of any kind. You'll be glad you did!

This beautiful porcelain box is topped with a lovely bouquet of porcelain flowers, perfect for holding rings, pins or other precious trinkets — and is yours absolutely free when you accept our no risk offer!

PLAY "LUCKY 7"

**Just scratch off the silver box with a coin.
Then check below to see the gifts you get.**

YES! I have scratched off the silver box. Please send me all the gifts for which I qualify. I understand I am under no obligation to purchase any books, as explained on the back and on the opposite page.

215 CIS A6NW
(U-SIL-R-01/97)

NAME

ADDRESS   APT.

CITY   STATE   ZIP

7	7	7	**WORTH FOUR FREE BOOKS PLUS A FREE PORCELAIN TRINKET BOX**
🍒	🍒	🍒	**WORTH THREE FREE BOOKS**
●	●	●	**WORTH TWO FREE BOOKS**
🔔	🔔	🍒	**WORTH ONE FREE BOOK**

Offer limited to one per household and not valid to current Silhouette Romance™ subscribers. All orders subject to approval.

© 1990 HARLEQUIN ENTERPRISES LIMITED   **PRINTED IN U.S.A.**

THE SILHOUETTE READER SERVICE™: HERE'S HOW IT WORKS

Accepting free books places you under no obligation to buy anything. You may keep the books and gift and return the shipping statement marked "cancel". If you do not cancel, about a month later we'll send you 6 additional novels, and bill you just $2.67 each plus 25¢ delivery per book and applicable sales tax, if any.* That's the complete price–and compared to cover prices of $3.25 each–quite a bargain! You may cancel at any time, but if you choose to continue, every month we'll send you 6 more books, which you may either purchase at the discount price…or return to us and cancel your subscription.

*Terms and prices subject to change without notice. Sales tax applicable in N.Y.

If offer card is missing, write to: Silhouette Reader Service, 3010 Walden Ave., PO Box 1867, Buffalo, NY 14240-1867

BUSINESS REPLY MAIL

FIRST-CLASS MAIL   PERMIT NO. 717   BUFFALO, NY

POSTAGE WILL BE PAID BY ADDRESSEE

SILHOUETTE READER SERVICE
3010 WALDEN AVE
PO BOX 1867
BUFFALO NY 14240-9952

NO POSTAGE
NECESSARY
IF MAILED
IN THE
UNITED STATES

ing a toddler is that it's not always you beaming while they take their first step or say 'Momma' for the first time. As a matter of fact, it can be downright lonely a lot of the time.''

Daniel frowned. "Lonely?" Rachel had looked like a Madonna out in the garden with Todd this morning. He'd thought so when he'd watched the two of them through his window. Rachel had been lonely out there? That couldn't be right. He'd sat in his office, feeling neglected. Surely he'd been the one all by himself?

Rachel removed her hands from Daniel's shoulders and hugged herself as the memories came.

It was probably close to eighty degrees in the study, yet Daniel fought the urge to shiver as the air hit the spot where Rachel's touch had just been.

"You remember how it was for you the other day when I got here, don't you?"

Daniel struggled to think, but all that came to him was how much he wanted Rachel to lean back over him again, maybe even wrap her arms around his neck instead of just resting her hands on his shoulders. A kiss on the back of his neck would certainly add to the visuals of the scene he was constructing as well.

Of course, should she choose to come around to his front and sit on his lap, kiss him properly... Daniel cleared his throat and said, "When?"

"When all you wanted me to do was talk? Don't you remember that? You didn't care what I talked about, just so you could hear another adult voice, you said."

"Oh, yeah. I have a vague memory of that." Vague memory, hah! Todd could stick his mashed banana-cereal combination breakfast goo into Daniel's ear before he'd admit how long yesterday had been. He'd simply put in time waiting for today and Rachel's arrival.

Rachel snorted. "It'll all come back to you the minute I leave, trust me."

Daniel was very much afraid that Rachel's observation was right on the money. It depressed the heck out of him. He couldn't think of anything to say, so he went back to work.

They labored side by side until three o'clock. Then, with Todd awake again, Rachel and Daniel took a break and ate the blueberry pie she'd baked earlier.

Daniel, even after the initiation he'd been through the past few weeks, still couldn't help but watch in horrified fascination as Todd's entire body gradually turned purple. "Look at that," he said, waving his fork in the child's general direction. "If I ever tried to describe this scene to anyone, I'd be accused of gross exaggeration."

"Not by anyone who'd ever been a parent," Rachel assured him. She sighed as a blueberry blob dropped off the tray and hit the floor. "It's been so long. Things come back, but sometimes not until it's too late."

"What do you mean?"

Rachel studied the grout lines of the ceramic-tiled floors and wondered how hard it would be to get blueberry stains out of them. "I remember now. When you give a kid something this messy to eat, you can save yourself a lot of grief by spreading a painter's tarp or an old vinyl tablecloth under the high chair. That way the floor doesn't get destroyed."

Daniel stared at her, impressed yet again. The woman was a wonder. Maybe he'd put off calling in the ad one more day and just see if with a little bit of extra time he couldn't charm Rachel around. He had it from any number of women that charm was his long suit, when he chose to exert it. Of course, Marie hadn't stayed under the influence all that long and Rachel—she seemed downright immune.

Oh, well. He'd have to work on it a little bit harder, that was all.

"That is an excellent idea. There's a discount store over by the mall. Tomorrow's Saturday, maybe Todd and I will head over in that direction and see what we can find."

Rachel nodded her approval. "Get the cheapest one they have. I'm sure it'll be fine." Then a thought hit. "You've driven with him in the car before, right?"

Daniel was too fascinated watching Todd paint himself purple to pay much attention. "Yeah, why?"

"Well, it's just that, I mean…you do buckle him into a car seat, don't you?"

Daniel chuckled and chose to tease her a bit. "Yes, Mother, I do."

Rachel recoiled, both horrified at his reaction and hurt at the same time. "I see people who leave their kids free bouncing around in the car while they're driving all the time when I'm out. It's so dangerous. I didn't know if you knew or not. I didn't mean to sound like your mother." This was terrible. Ron had accused her of treating him as a child, too. But when you were around children all day and all night, it was tough to switch gears. She'd found herself cutting off Ron's crust one day back when Mark had been a little bit older than Todd. Cutting the crust off a grown man's sandwich, for God's sake.

But darn, Rachel didn't have a single maternal thought when it came to Daniel. Not one. "I'm sorry."

Daniel eyed her with amazement, Todd and his purple sludge temporarily forgotten. "Rachel, I was kidding. I don't mind your asking. It's just that somehow or another, I did know about car seats. But I might not have, you couldn't be sure. Like the tarp under the high chair, I'd have been very grateful for your having told me, had that been the case.''

He was just being polite, she knew it. She also felt like an idiot. ''I still didn't mean to be demeaning or give the impression I thought you needed all my sage counsel and advice or anything.''

''I do need your sage counsel and advice.'' And Daniel was particularly interested in the anything else she'd referred to. But he'd obviously touched a nerve and needed to do some fence-mendings before he thought about pursuing the *anythings*. Reluctantly Daniel set his fork down. Damn, that pie had been good. He reached over and took Rachel's hands in his. ''Hey, I'm not upset, okay? If Todd hadn't climbed right into his car seat and looked so expectantly at me, waiting for me to buckle the straps that first time we went out in the car, I probably would never have stopped to think about it. It's just a fluke that got me started doing it, that's all. A fluke, all right? Now smile for me,'' he coaxed. ''Come on.''

She smiled sheepishly, her eyes downcast.

The woman was adorable and there was nothing he wanted more than to kiss her. ''Know what?''

''What?''

''Your teeth are blue.''

''Oh, yeah? Well, so are yours.''

''Is that right?''

Rachel nodded. ''Yeah, that's right.''

Daniel grinned and ran his tongue around his teeth.

Rachel stared, fascinated. ''So's your tongue.''

''You got a smart mouth, lady.''

"And I suppose you think you can do something about it, too."

It was an ages-old childish challenge, yet Daniel couldn't resist rising to the bait. "Maybe I can at that." He stood, placed his palms down on the oak tabletop and leaned over the table. "Here, I'll clean your teeth for you." And he kissed her, running his tongue along her lips until she parted them slightly.

"Oh, God," he moaned, pulling back briefly.

"Daniel?" she whispered, shaken.

Oh, man, talk about being unprofessional. It was his final thought before his circuits fried and all he could think about was getting the damn table out from between the middle of them. He grasped Rachel by her forearm and pulled her around the edge of the kitchen table. Then he tucked her up nice and close against him and anchored her there with arms that suddenly felt as hard as steel.

"You feel so good next to me," he breathed in her ear. His exhalation caught Rachel's hair and it fluttered gently around his face, beating him almost senseless with the strands of silk. "And you smell so good."

Rachel responded rather inanely considering her sudden new position, "I don't see how I could. I don't wear perfume in the fall, the bees, you know."

Daniel had no idea what she was talking about and couldn't have cared less. "Perfume? I'm not talking about that stuff. It makes me sneeze. You smell like baked chicken and blueberry pie—good enough to eat, that's how you smell."

How was she supposed to respond to that? A woman of her advanced years should know, Rachel was sure. Then again, maybe not. How many men were there in the world that got turned on by blue teeth?

He started nibbling on her earlobe while she pondered answerless questions until Rachel barely avoided squealing at the gentle nips Daniel administered. As it was, her voice squeaked only slightly when she spoke. "We need to, um, clean up Todd, Daniel."

"We will. In a couple of minutes. Put your arms around me."

She did. He felt wonderful, strong, all male. Rachel conveniently forgot she'd been silently complaining about his maleness just that morning. Now she only recognized that he was excitingly firm under her touch, not soft like a desk jockey ought to feel. There was not an ounce of flab on his body and Rachel felt deliciously feminine crushed as she was against all that blatant, hard masculinity.

Todd banged his cup and Rachel jumped.

Feminine, but stupid, that's what she was. Just as she'd been with Ron all those years before. Had she learned nothing from that experience? What was she doing standing in Daniel's kitchen necking in front of a toddler? Where was her common sense? "Daniel, you need to let me go."

"I will. Just give me a couple of seconds." Rachel was absolutely right, Daniel told himself. Todd was getting restless in his confinement, he was demanding their attention. Oops, there went the milk. "No, Todd, no." He needed to let her go. And he would, just as soon as he could figure out how to get his brain to transmit the command down to his arms in such a manner that those traitorous appendages would actually listen. There was a failure, a massive breakdown somewhere in the system between here and there and his arms simply refused to release the woman they held.

Daniel would have laughed, only it really wasn't
funny. In the dim recesses of his mind, he knew, he *knew*
that holding her now probably meant not holding her
later. It was too soon for any of this stuff. Way too soon,
and acting on that knowledge would no doubt kill him.
Daniel found her mouth and kissed her once more.
"Turn around," he said.

"What?" Rachel's voice sounded fuzzy, as if she was
having a hard time focusing on what he was saying.

"Turn around so that your back is to me."

"Why?" Now she sounded confused.

"Then you'll be in a position to peel my hands off of
you. I can't seem to make them move. They like it right
where they are."

"That's silly." But she blushed.

Daniel shrugged in a helpless gesture. "Yeah, but
that's the way it is. What's a guy supposed to do?"

So Rachel twisted in his grasp and tugged his hands
off her midriff. The amount of reluctance she had to
overcome to perform the task was truly irritating.

Frankly Daniel thought she'd put more little gyra-
tions into the task than absolutely necessary and he was
hurting as a result, but the woman was free. Let her try
to complain. Daniel took a deep breath and exhaled
slowly, ordering his rebellious body back into line as he
did so. Gradually he felt control returning. He ordered
his hand to brush the hair back off his face and it actually complied. He decided not to press his luck by asking anything else of his body, so Daniel stayed right
where he was—although he did lean back against the
table in an affectation of nonchalance.

He was pleased to hear Rachel's voice sounding a little thin when she spoke. Clearly she had not been unaf-
fected by what had passed between them and Daniel

hated the idea of suffering alone. He was not so happy, however, with her words.

"I should probably get going. There are things that need doing." Exactly which things, she couldn't say right offhand, but some would no doubt come to mind the moment the smoke cleared out of her brain.

"Like what?"

"Well, uh—"

"You can't leave yet." Daniel waved his hand around to encompass the kitchen. "You wouldn't desert me now, would you? Look at this mess. Never mind the mess, look at that child! You couldn't be so cruel. I wouldn't even know where to begin." It was only a slight exaggeration, Daniel thought as he grimaced at the sight of his nephew. "You can't stand there with a straight face and tell me that's not a two-man, um, person job."

Rachel studied Todd and sighed. He was right. There'd be no escaping just yet. "All right. Start the water going in the sink while I get his shirt off."

"This sink right here? You're going to bathe him in the kitchen sink?"

"It's closest. You don't want this stuff dripping from here to kingdom come, do you? Blueberry stains permanently, I think. You've got beige carpeting in this place."

"All right, but it doesn't seem right to me."

"Trust me, it's done all the time. I know lots of kids who were bathed in the kitchen sink and grew up to enjoy almost normal adulthoods. Oh, and we need a towel, too."

Daniel went to do her bidding and Rachel approached Todd in his high chair. She studied him briefly, trying to decide on the best angle of attack. Finally she just tackled him head-on. "Now, Todd, you just keep your sticky little mitts to yourself, you hear me?" Rachel quickly grabbed the hem of his T-shirt and yanked it over his head, sealing his hands inside the fabric before pulling it completely free and stepping aside.

"You should see the look on your face. Absolutely priceless." Daniel set the towel he'd fetched next to the sink, checked the water temperature with the back of his hand and turned off the tap.

"Oh, yeah? Well, you get him next. I'm going to take a picture of your expression when you've got to hold him and frame it, too."

"Me? I thought you were going to do this. I got all the stuff ready. Look, I even remembered a bar of soap. You didn't think of that, did you?"

"Well, aren't you Mr. Wonderful? Now come over here and, while I hold his hands so he doesn't slime you, you grab him around the waist. Rotate him as you pull him out of the high chair so that he's facing out. Then he can't get you."

"Right. Got it." But Daniel stood there, eyeing his nephew dubiously. "You're sure about this?"

"Unless you've got a better idea?"

Daniel took a deep breath. "All right, here goes nothing." He stepped forward. "Wait a minute, I'm taking off my own shirt before I get involved any further in this." And he did just that.

Rachel deeply regretted the action. Her pulse, which she'd just managed to settle down was now in danger of pumping her life's blood supply out the top of her head. Her mouth went dry and she suddenly felt as if her tongue was going to choke her. Honest to God, she'd never seen a chest like that. Certainly Ron hadn't been blessed with one, and he'd been a football player—a starter even, which was why she, the gullible little cheerleader Rachel had been back in high school, had fallen for all his lines and ploys.

Daniel noticed Rachel's eyes widen as he approached the high chair shirtless now. He felt a glimmer of self-satisfaction. He'd done nothing to earn his broad shoulders and tapered waist, although he admitted to fine-tuning them a bit with a weight workout every now and again. No, his body had been a genetic gift from his mother and father. His physique had little or nothing to do with who and what he was, but Daniel certainly wasn't averse to using it to his advantage when it suited his purposes. Daniel flexed slightly, subtlety being the key. It wouldn't do to be obvious. Rachel would know. He almost smiled when her eyes widened further, but he managed to maintain a suitably serious demeanor. "Okay, I'm ready. You get behind him and hold his hands. I'll loosen the tray and tackle him from the front."

Their maneuvering was deft, their task accomplished with minimal fuss. Rachel stripped Todd of his shorts and diaper while Daniel grasped him under the arms and held him out, his little legs dangling and pumping in the air.

Rachel was amazed with Daniel's muscle power. Holding such a heavy weight out from your body with no support other than your arm muscles must require tremendous strength. She remembered clearly the hard feel of those arms when they'd held her moments before.

Arms like those wouldn't loosen anything they didn't want loose.

It was a scary thought. Exciting, too.

"Let's get him into the sink."

"My pleasure."

Together they moved to the sink, Daniel carefully setting the child into the water. "Sit down, Todd," he instructed and helped Todd fold his legs as he went down so he'd fit into the sink.

So, Rachel thought as she observed, he's got his strength completely under control. Those arms are capable of gentleness and kindness. His care in his motions was obvious.

It was a comforting thought. Reassuring. Beguiling. Totally irrelevant, at least for her.

Rachel wrapped up the rest of the blueberry pie in plastic film and found a place for it in the refrigerator. She scraped the dishes they'd used and put them into the dishwasher, setting it for Rinse, then wiped off the table and countertop. She'd have to wait until the sink was vacated to clean the high chair tray. That needed a good dunking in soapy water. Through it all, Rachel watched Daniel and Todd. Daniel managed to make the bath a game. He tickled Todd's toes and pulled off his nose, showing it to the child in the form of the tip of his thumb poking through his folded fingers before pretending to stick the appendage back on his nephew's face.

Todd laughed uproariously. Daniel, thoroughly into the horseplay with eyes sparkling, was caught up in the infectious sound and laughed himself.

Men, thought Rachel—only she couldn't dredge up her usual rancor when she thought of the opposite sex and their inherent immaturity. They never grow up. They're all little boys at heart.

Funny how the very same thoughts that had brought on anger and aching before now precipitated a smile.

"Ready to get out, champ?" Daniel asked, totally aware of every furtive glance Rachel had shot his way during the bathing process. "You stay in there much longer and you'll turn into a prune. Nothing very macho about that, is there, big guy? Can you hand me that towel, Rachel, honey?"

Rachel stared at his back, momentarily frozen. He'd called her honey. Probably it was one of those terms that dripped off a man's tongue just like its namesake, but still—

Daniel held one hand out behind him. The other steadied Todd as he stood in the sink, water dripping off his pudgy little body and swirling down the drain at his feet. "Hold still, Todd. Rachel?"

"Hmm? Oh! The towel. Here. Put the plug back in until you've got him out, Daniel."

"Todd! I said hold still! I'll have you out in just a second, as soon as I get you wrapped up in this towel. Be still or you're going to slip and get hurt."

Rachel reached around Daniel and settled the plug back into the drain. Immediately Todd settled down. Instead of moving away, she stayed close for a moment, breathing in Daniel's masculine scent. God, she was losing her mind. She had no instincts for self-preservation whatsoever. It was probably middle-age crisis. Why not? She could add it to her empty nest syndrome and her I-must-be-no-good-and-worthless-since-not-even-my-husband-wants-me-anymore low self-esteem complex. She took one more deep sniff before managing to move away.

Daniel looked at her curiously, Todd safely out of the sink now. Roughing the kid up with the towel, he asked, "Why'd you put the plug back?"

Rachel reached into the sink and loosened it once more. "He was getting upset. I heard someplace kids worry about going down the drain with the water, so I always left the plug in until after Mark was out."

Daniel looked amazed by such an idea. "Todd can't fit down the drain."

"He doesn't know that," she retorted.

Daniel looked from Rachel to Todd. The boy had calmed down and was playing peekaboo with the corner of the towel and Daniel. He shifted his gaze back to Rachel. "You're right. Thanks for pointing that out."

Daniel bent his head slightly, meaning to give her a friendly kiss of appreciation. Nothing heavy, he promised himself.

Rachel saw his intent and stepped back. "Everything seems to be under control now. I've really got to run now. Um, bye!" She took off like the coward she felt.

"Wait!" He reached for her, but she danced back. She was almost out of the kitchen now. "When are you coming back?" Damn, this was frustrating. She'd spooked for some reason and he couldn't reach her to calm her, not without leaving Todd naked on the kitchen counter. He might fall and get hurt. Daniel had to stay right there. "Rachel?"

"Oh, I'm not really sure, Daniel. Not for a while." The words stuck in her throat, but she forced herself to say them. Self-preservation, she told herself. It was time to become part of the me-generation and think of herself. Numero uno, that was her. "You really need to get that ad called in, you know. Your life would be so much easier."

Daniel watched her retreating back with a sinking feeling in his chest. His life was a bloody disaster. The one person he knew of who could have set it right had just taken off out the door and it was probably all his own fault for making her nervous. Well, damn.

He sighed. "Come on, Todd, you need a clean diaper. One of these days you and I have to sit down and discuss potty training, but I guess at your age that would be jumping my fences too soon again, wouldn't it?"

Patience. It had never been his long suit.

Chapter Seven

"Hello?"

"Rachel? It's your long lost sister, Eileen. You remember me. I'm the one just to your right in every family photo portrait our parents ever had taken."

Uh-oh. For some reason or another, Eileen was in her martyr mode. Rachel knew there'd be no escape for her until Eileen had vented all her complaints and accusations. Rachel plunked herself down on the living room sofa, put her feet up on the coffee table listing now from years of similar abuse and reached for her diet cola. She was now prepared to listen. "Since Mom and Dad only had the two of us, you were tough to miss in those pictures, although you're wrong about always being on the right. The one on Mom and Dad's living-room mantel has you on the left and I think I recall another one where the photographer put you directly behind me. I think he was going for depth of field in that one."

"Oh, shut up. I was there someplace, wasn't I? I figured you must have forgotten about me since it's been a month of Sundays since you've bothered to call."

Yes, indeed. Eileen was on the warpath and judging by the opening salvos, in rare form tonight. "It hasn't been *that* long, Eileen. Only a couple of days."

Her sister's voice shot right back over the telephone wire. "Oh, no. More than a couple."

Rachel sighed. "Okay, so how many has it been? Three? Four? No more than that, I'm positive. And whatever the actual count is, I apologize, but I've been sort of busy."

Rachel doubted she'd get off that easily. Eileen was in no mood to buy easy excuses. Sometimes Rachel felt as if she'd been born with two mothers. And sure enough, here came more guilt to add to the trip.

"Too busy to call your own sister? Your very own sister who let you buy her silence with only half of a Kit Kat bar the night you let Ron into the house even though neither Mom nor Dad was home and it was forbidden?

"I have to tell you, Rachel, I expected better when I expressly requested that you call me back with a report on the hunk who crashed in your front yard. He and the kid could have been faking an injury until somebody gullible enough to kidnap came out. For all I knew, what with you being so spacey and unable to remember my street number without looking it up in your address book, they wouldn't have known where to send the ransom request and you could have been sitting around all trussed up somewhere waiting for a payoff that would never come."

Rachel sipped her cola and closed her eyes. "That's silly, even for you. And I know how to get to your house, it's the third house on the left on the second block after you turn right off of whatever street that is two blocks after you pass Main. I just can't remember the street name or your house number right offhand. How often do I mail you anything, after all?''

"So what would you do? Offer to drive your kidnappers over?''

"If necessary, yes. But I didn't get kidnapped! You were the one who told me to go down there. It was a great way to meet a new neighbor, you said.''

"And you were supposed to call me back and let me know what happened,'' Eileen said explosively in her ear. "So,'' she said and Rachel could hear the struggle for control in her voice. "Was I right?''

"About what?'' Rachel inquired, having difficulty following the conversation.

"Is he your neighbor? Is he as good-looking up close as you thought he'd be? Is he available? Was it his kid?''

"Um, let's see. Yes. Yes. Yes. Sort of.''

"Rachel, you're making me crazy,'' Eileen warned. "Which one of the above were you answering with the sort of? Now I can't remember what I asked you last. Hang on just a second. Carrie, put that back in the refrigerator. Dinner's almost ready. Rachel? Tell me about the guy. Is he divorced or what?''

Rachel took another contemplative sip of her drink. "No, he's just a nice guy who, through no fault of his own, is caught in a sticky situation. If you want to know the truth, I feel sorry for him.'' And a lot of other less understandable and excusable emotions as well.

"Sorry! Why sorry?''

Rachel looked out the window. Closing in on six o'clock and still light outside. That wouldn't last long. Winter was so dark and depressing. Sometimes she felt as if the rest of her life would be spent in the cold and dark. Rachel couldn't help but wonder how Daniel was facing up to the coming long hours of dark—or was he so busy surviving on a day-to-day basis he hadn't given the coming seasonal changes a thought? She inhaled deeply to dispel her melancholia, then went on to describe Daniel's situation to Eileen.

"Oh, wow."

Rachel put her head back against the sofa. "Yeah. It's bad, I can tell you that. I ran into the two of them at the grocery store last night. He was buying canned soup for dinner. Canned soup. I felt so bad, I went down and spent the day helping out, made dinner for lunch so I'd know they'd have at least one decent meal today." God, she sounded so altruistic. Well, she *had* wanted to make a good meal for them, but Rachel wasn't sure her motives had been all that wonderful and pure. Mostly, she'd wanted to impress Daniel.

"That was very nice of you, Rachel."

Well, Eileen bought it, at least.

"But tell me about *him*. Is he hot? Did your little heart go pitter-patter? Did he grab you, toss you down on the kitchen table and ravish you? Come on, anything happen that I should know about but Mom and Dad shouldn't?"

Or maybe not. Rachel gripped the phone and leaned forward, curling her upper body over her legs. "He offered me a job, Eileen. Watching Todd and helping him out in his office when Todd napped."

"How perfect! I can't believe you found a job without even having to go out and look. And talk about convenient. The commute will be practically nil and you won't even have to add majorly to your wardrobe. This is wonderful. Of course you snapped at it."

"No. In fact, I've decided not to go back at all, not even as a temporary kind of thing until he finds somebody else."

"What? I cannot believe my ears! Why not?"

"There's just something funny about the whole deal."

"Like what? You think he'd take advantage of the situation? Did he come on to you? Wait—hang on. Carrie, I mean it. Get out of the kitchen until I call you for supper." There was a short pause, then, "Okay, I can talk again. Now let's think about this for a moment, Rachel. If this guy's as good-looking as you say, couldn't you just relax and enjoy a fling kind of thing with him? It's not like Mark's around and you have to worry about setting a good example anymore or anything."

Rachel was appalled. This was her own sister talking like that! "After what I went through with Ron?"

"You're a lot older now, sweetcakes. One would assume you've learned about birth control by this point in your life. After all, you managed to not get pregnant again after Mark."

That was true enough, but even so— "Listen, Eileen, to tell you the truth, the reason I don't want to go back there is because when I'm around him I find myself thinking I'd settle for a fling."

"Really? Wow. Coming from you, that's quite a compliment. He *must* be hot."

Rachel watched a leaf drift past the living room window. The beginning of the end. "God, yes. He's gorgeous. But in my heart of hearts, I know I wouldn't like myself much afterward."

"Hmm. I can see your point, I guess," Eileen admitted reluctantly. "But if you took the job, maybe you could make yourself so indispensable, he'd realize he couldn't possibly get along without you and offer to marry you. What do you think?''

"I think you're nuts and I think I don't want anybody to marry me because I make their life run smoother. I want somebody to love me and want to marry me for myself, not because they were afraid of running out of matched socks or clean underwear."

"First you hook them, then you teach them to match socks. Over the years Bob's gotten quite good at it."

Rachel snorted in a very unladylike manner. "Yeah, well, Ron never did get the knack." Rachel sighed so gustily, she felt her bangs move in the resultant breeze. "There's no doubt I could make myself indispensable. Todd's darling, but a handful and Daniel looks at me like a drowning man eyeing a rescue tube. But you know what? I've been there, I've done all that. Now I just want to be loved, damn it. Loved, do you hear?"

"Holy mackerel, Rachel, don't fall apart. Of course I hear you. You're yelling into the phone. Hang on a second, I need to make sure Carrie's not anywhere around." Eileen all but whispered into the phone then. "All right, you've convinced me. An affair would be tacky, at least for you. Forget I mentioned it."

How depressing to be proven right. Rachel suddenly realized she'd been hoping to have Eileen tell her she'd been worrying over nothing, that this was all some preordained meant-to-be twist of fate and her destiny lay with Daniel and all he needed was a little convincing. Darn it anyway.

"So what are you going to do instead?"

How like her sister to be so practical. "I guess I'll start checking around, see if I can find a computer class someplace." It didn't sound nearly as interesting as it had only a short week ago. Somehow that nine-to-five job she'd lusted after as the obvious remedy to the previous eighteen years of fourteen or more hour days had lost some of its luster.

"Yes, that's what I'll do. Find a computer class and then start in with the want ads." She wondered if she'd see Daniel's ad in there. Who would respond to his ad? Someone who could be trusted with Todd? She hadn't meant for it to happen, but she was already attached to the child. Daniel had better be very thorough in his interview process. If he let any weirdos in there to take care of that little baby, he'd hear about it from her, make no mistake. Hmm, maybe she ought to volunteer to help in the interviewing, rule out some of the more obvious psychos bound to apply for such a cushy setup.

Eileen interrupted her thoughts. "Listen, Rachel, I've got to go. Dinner's ready and Carrie's about to eat the tabletop. The high school girl's swim team is already practicing and that always gives her a hollow leg, so I need to get this served up. Let me know what happens."

"All right, I will. Give Carrie my love."

"I will. Bye, now."

"Bye-bye."

Rachel replaced the receiver and thought about checking up on Mark. No, she decided. Her son would only be irritated with what he'd see as maternal interference. Either that, or he'd badger her some more over the money he'd asked her to send.

Should she break down and send him some? Rachel nibbled a fingernail as she debated.

Naw, it would set a bad precedent to bail him out this early in the year. He needed to learn to budget his funds.

That was right, she was sure of it.

Wasn't it?

Maybe she'd send just a twenty.

No, that would undo everything she'd said about living with the consequences of your actions. God knows, she'd lived with hers. She'd never regret having had Mark, but some of the rest of the consequences of that long ago prom night she could have done quite nicely without. Resolutely Rachel walked out of the room. Cave in on this and next thing you know, he'd be calling to inform her of impending grandmotherhood and by the way, could she support the three of them while he finished school? No, thank you.

She'd reached the kitchen when she decided to wait another week before sending him a ten. And a box of condoms. That resolved, Rachel looked for the Community Education brochure, finally locating it in the kitchen trash. Paging through the flyer, she homed right in on a *Computers, Friend or Foe?* class listing. It said the class would specialize in making the uninitiated literate in computerese in virtually no time at all. Just what she needed. Rachel left the booklet open to that page and set the pamphlet on the countertop. She'd call tomorrow and register. Scooping the rest of the trash back into the bin, Rachel shut it back under the sink.

Rachel studied the closed door as she realized she'd been living there almost one whole week and, not counting moving boxes, had yet to fill her first full bag of garbage. One was indeed a lonely number. Rachel still didn't have a full load of colored or whites to wash yet, either, but was going to have do laundry anyway. She was running out of clothes. Depressed, she rinsed out her glass and set it upside down on the drain board, turned off the kitchen light and trailed her way slowly down the hall to her too-quiet bedroom.

The bedside clock proclaimed it to be barely eight o'clock. She'd be up even before the crack of dawn if she went to bed now. Looking around at the four walls doing their best to close in on her, Rachel decided that, for a rousing finale to an almost overwhelmingly exciting evening, she'd shower and pray to God there was something decent on television that would help occupy her while she lay on her bed leafing through the old magazines Eileen had given her.

Daniel had his feet up on his desk and the telephone receiver to his ear. It was early Monday afternoon, Todd was in his crib napping, the house was still standing after a rather hairy weekend and Daniel suspected, this was probably about as good as it got.

Unfortunately Rachel hadn't called over the weekend to rescind her refusal, which was really too darn bad. She'd have been perfect for the job. She always brightened up the place. The house felt . . . empty since Rachel had left last Friday. He could almost hear the echoes of Rachel's delighted laughter as she'd played with Todd the Friday before.

Daniel frowned. How ridiculous. He was getting maudlin. Of course he missed her. She'd been a big help, gotten a lot done. Then he remembered John McEndoe on the other end of the phone and sat up straighter, listening and trying to catch what he'd missed without sounding stupid.

He should not be down. In fact, he should be happy, happy, happy. Daniel had felt compelled to go ahead and put an ad up on the bulletin boards at both Saint Mary's College and the South Bend branch of Indiana University for day-care just that morning and as far as his new business was concerned, an actual, honest to God real client was calling him this afternoon. It was kismet. And although he'd have preferred his kismet with Rachel in the starring role, Daniel was rapidly learning one didn't always get what one preferred in this life. So he'd make sure the girl he hired from St. Mary's or IUSB had a nice laugh, that was all. Or he'd order a laugh track to play when he was lonely. One or the other, but he wouldn't pine over Rachel. Absolutely not.

"Yes, John, I understand. Most accounting firms reserve sampling for the larger auto dealers. I promise an accurate and complete physical inventory of every car on your lot as part of my examination of your books. I'll take nothing for granted." He leaned back in his chair, listening.

"Yes, certainly." Daniel nodded his head, although John couldn't see his agreement. Suddenly he sat up.

"Uh, next week?" Frantically he thought but nothing came. "Well, I might be able to squeeze it in." Oh, man, how? But he needed this job, he really did. "In fact, I'm sure I can get to it. Wednesday morning? I'll be there."

Daniel hung up the phone. He felt dazed. What to do? No way would he have interviewed and found a proper candidate to watch Todd in nine days. The phone rang again. Automatically Daniel reached for it.

"Daniel Van Scott," he answered. "Bob Rothman? You're kidding! My God, man, I haven't seen hide nor hair of you in years. What's going down in your neck of the woods? Now that I think about it, how did you know how to reach me...?"

"Is that right? Yeah, I did see Jimmy a few weeks back. He gave you my card? Man, that thing I slipped him was a train wreck, all scratched up and written all over. I promised him one of my new ones as soon as they came in. Hey, I'll see that you get one, too. Jimmy Halbook, how about that." Daniel put his feet on his desk again and leaned back in his chair. He put his free hand behind his head and stretched. "Small world, I guess, huh . . . ?"

"No, I hadn't heard you'd bought a franchise. Up to five stores now? Congratulations, big guy! That's really something. . . ."

"Yeah, yeah, I'm just getting started myself. . . ."

"Oh, that's what Jimmy told you? Sure I could. I'd love to. I've got an auto dealership on for next week. As soon as I'm done with that? Great. Good talking to you, man. I'll be in touch."

By the time Daniel hung up the second time, he was punch-drunk. Two clients in the space of about fifteen minutes. Unbelievable. He'd have to remember to send Jimmy a little something for sending the business his way. A box of cigars or something. Did Jimmy smoke? Who cared? It was the thought that counted.

But there was still nobody to watch Todd while he was off counting cars and then hamburger patties and bags of frozen french fries at Bob's. He chewed his bottom lip, drummed the fingers of his right hand thoughtfully on the desktop. Finally he wadded up several sheets of paper and shot them at the wastebasket, making two of three baskets.

He nodded to himself. Rachel was the only solution. She simply had to come through for him. He'd make her see reason, that was all. He *had* to.

Daniel decided he'd call her the next morning. No, he'd go down there in person, that was it. Rachel was a softy at heart. She'd never be able to turn him down face-to-face.

At least he didn't think so.

No, he was right. He'd have Todd with him, after all. She was a sucker for little kids, that had been obvious from the start. He just had to explain it all right. He'd always been good with words. A stab of guilt pricked his conscience when he remembered how lonely playing Mom to Todd had made Rachel feel. Then he remembered how well they'd worked together caring for Todd. How much they'd laughed. And then there was that kiss...

There was nothing more to decide. He *needed* Rachel, in more ways than he cared to think about. Instead he spent the rest of the afternoon planning exactly how he'd plead his case to her.

The day marched on until, inevitably and as regular as clockwork, night came. Then, in slightly under twelve hours, morning blossomed. Daniel was awake to watch the pink and orange petals of dawn unfold in the eastern sky, his mind still whirring along.

"Beautiful," he murmured to himself as he stared out his bedroom window. "Now if the day will only continue as it has begun." Daniel figured it wouldn't hurt to put a bit of a bug into the ultimate mover and shaker's ear. "God, please let Rachel listen and be reasonable about this when I see her. I know she wants to get on with her life after her divorce, but this is important, okay? Really important." Daniel found himself engaging more and more frequently in these brief snippets of prayerful supplication. Nothing like parenthood, he guessed, to firm up a person's faith foundation.

Unable to fall back asleep, Daniel dressed in sport shorts and sneakers, and that was all. "If somebody else was living here with me," he told himself as he snuck down the hall and past Todd's closed door, "I'd go out for a nice long run. But as it is..." He shrugged philosophically. "Oh well. Maybe in my next lifetime."

Instead he went out to the living room and the exercise bike he'd purchased over the weekend. Damn, but Sarah would have a heart attack and die all over again if she could see the exercise bike set up in her living room. Unfortunately there was no place else for it. He set the TV to CNN and the bike to simulate hill riding, then mounted the thing. Daniel rode through several bombings, a couple of murders and an Ebola outbreak before he called it quits. Todd would be awakening soon and Daniel needed to shower first.

An hour and a half later, Daniel, armed with Todd, felt ready to face the lioness in her den.

"Come on, Todd," he instructed the toddler, "let's go see if Rachel's home." He was too chicken to call her first for fear she'd come up with some handy excuse not to see them. So, he made sure his answering machine would pick up any calls and led Todd out the door, holding his hand as he negotiated the step down to the porch and then the three more that let them off at sidewalk level.

Rachel was home and looking deliciously mussed, Daniel discovered. He barely refrained from manually checking to make sure his mouth wasn't hanging open, but, damn, she looked good with her hair all messy and one hand clutching her thin cotton robe closed up by her neck.

Made him wonder what she wore underneath. He wasn't going to be the one to tell her that the morning light was filtering right through that robe and presenting him with a perfect outline of her body.

"Good morning, Rachel." Whatever it was she had on under her cover-up was either nonexistent or as flimsy as all get-out. His throat tightened as he tried to imagine her without the robe and he had to swallow before he could say, "Todd, say good morning to Rachel."

"Good mo-mo-mo—" Todd gave it a manly effort, but despite several gallant attempts, failed to pull it off.

Rachel beamed at him anyway. "Good morning to you, too, sir. What are the two of you doing out so bright and early?"

Daniel cleared his throat. "The fact of the matter is, we came out specifically to see you, Rachel."

Rachel's heart fluttered around a bit in her chest at the thought of Daniel purposely seeking out her company, but her momma hadn't given birth to any stupid babies. She decided to play it cool. "Really? Well, then, maybe you both ought to come in. I was about to make some pancakes. I was thinking about whole wheat, but I also picked up some buckwheat at the health food store yesterday, if you'd prefer that."

"You were going to go to all that trouble for just one person? Wow, I'm impressed."

No, of course she hadn't been going to. Now that they had shown up on her doorstep, though, she would. Filling them up on fresh orange juice and whole grain pancakes would help assuage the guilt she felt whenever she thought of Daniel in the canned soup aisle and her refusal of his job offer, that was all. "It's no big deal," she assured him, even though her heart had started force-feeding blood to the rest of her body the minute she'd opened her door and found him there. She could feel it pounding through her temples. "Come on in."

Daniel ushered Todd through her front door and up the long flight of stairs to the second floor. He looked around her living room. Any packing boxes were out of sight and although he knew she'd been there only a short time, the apartment had a warm, homey feel to it. The sofa was large, one of those overstuffed models, its blue color slightly faded. The coffee table in front of it also bore marks of use and all but groaned under a stack of magazines. The windows had sheers with blue side panels tied back with red ropy things sporting tassels on their ends. There were a couple of tall brass lamps sitting on sturdy wooden end tables and a tweedy-looking kind of wing chair positioned at a right angle to the sofa. Not ritzy, but all in all a room a man could be comfortable in.

"To be honest, Todd and I already had a bowl of cereal this morning," Daniel admitted reluctantly.

Rachel immediately pooh-poohed that. "That won't stick with you all morning. Come into the kitchen. We can talk while I cook."

Daniel decided to wait until they'd eaten to discuss his business and, damn, but the woman knew how to cook. He leaned back in his chair and smiled contentedly at Todd. Rachel had propped him up on the phone directories she'd received last week and then she'd gone through her winter box to find a long woolen neck scarf to wrap around Todd's middle and then around the chair back to keep him from slipping off the chair while they sat there. Todd was doodling in the syrup left on his empty but still sticky plate.

"That was wonderful," Daniel told her.

She had no reason to doubt his sincerity. He'd eaten three batches.

"Thank you, Rachel."

"You're welcome." Rachel collected the plate in front of him. "Now, what did you want to talk about?"

Daniel sat up. It was now or never. "Well, I got some really good news yesterday, but the thing is—"

Rachel listened with a sinking heart as Daniel described his problem. She hadn't *really* thought he'd come down just because he'd missed her. Not really. So why did she feel so downcast that all he wanted was her services again? It was silly. Suddenly tired of his rambling explanation, Rachel cut Daniel off midsentence. "Fine, I'll do it, Daniel."

Daniel blinked owlishly. "Excuse me?"

"I said I'd sit for Todd a few more times while you go count cars and french fries."

"Oh. Well. Good." He'd been prepared to argue a lot longer and Daniel was at a loss as to what to say now. "Uh, thank you. I really appreciate this. I don't know how else I'd pull this off without you. You're a godsend, Rachel, honestly you are. You, um, want to come to the park with us for a while?"

Rachel shook her head. It wouldn't do to get too close when there was no future there. "No, I've got things to do. You two go ahead. I'll see you Wednesday morning, a week from tomorrow, bright and early."

It took her fifteen more minutes, but she managed to shoo them out the door. Then Rachel sulked for the rest of the morning. Her mood was a little extreme, but she figured she deserved a good wallow in a bit of self-pity. Just once, she wanted to be wanted for herself. Just once.

Chapter Eight

Rachel allowed herself a couple of hours to brood, then declared it time to get on with her life. She'd wallowed in enough self-pity immediately following the divorce to know it didn't get you anything but a headache. Basically an optimist, she called and registered for the computer literacy class, then spent the next eight days attempting to convince herself that her life would soon be back on track, that whatever little side trails she'd somehow gotten herself detoured on in several areas of her life would soon switch back to the main path and everything would be okay.

Everything will be okay. Rachel repeated it while she did laundry. Not that the clothes were stacked to the ceiling—far from it, but she only had one clean pair of panties and a single brassiere left. Running out of underwear did not appeal. After washing her pathetic little load, Rachel decided to go out and buy several more pair. Build her stock up to a two-week supply. Then she wouldn't feel so stupid pulling her few little items out of that great big machine down at the Laundromat while everyone else strained under their massive family-size loads.

Everything will be okay. Standing in the grocery store, Rachel turned her head as she passed the soup aisle. She refused to buy a can of soup for her dinner just because she was eating by herself and it wasn't worth getting the pans dirty just for one.

Maybe for lunch she'd allow some convenience food, but not dinner. She was worth more than that. So every evening of those eight days, Rachel made a production of setting the table with her single place setting and cooking real food. A small piece of orange roughy one night, half a chicken breast another. Real dinner food. The butcher came to recognize her as she had to request all her meat items repackaged. Nothing came wrapped in servings for one.

Everything will be okay. On Tuesday, Rachel put two five dollar bills into an envelope and mailed it to Mark along with some literature she'd found on safe sex. He'd have to buy his own condoms. Rachel had been down that aisle in the drugstore twice and hadn't been able to work up the courage to walk up to the cash register with them. As if it would somehow make up for her cowardice, she pledged to herself that she'd bake some chocolate chip cookies, maybe Thursday, and ship them down to his dorm room. If she kept Mark's and his vegetarian girlfriend's mouths busy, maybe they wouldn't get around to the other stuff. That was the maternal brain for you, always hoping for the best.

"Do you suppose Daniel keeps a supply of condoms?" she asked her sister, Eileen, during one of their phone conversations. Once her mind had latched on to the subject with Mark, somehow her brain had made a connection with Daniel and then his love life—a subject she was probably far better off not wondering about. Unfortunately, once she'd started, it was tough to turn off the switch.

"You mean like next to his bed in his nightstand drawer like in the movies?"

"Yeah." Ron hadn't wanted to take any chances. After a false alarm when Mark was four, Ron had taken care of things permanently. There'd been no condoms in their bedroom. Her ex-husband hadn't considered them secure enough, as though another baby by her would be tantamount to the plague. But what about today's singles? What did they do?

"You could look when you're there tomorrow."

Rachel turned scarlet just thinking about it. "Oh, I couldn't!"

"Sure you could," Eileen assured her. "In the afternoon while you're baby-sitting. Who's going to know? Daniel will be out doing whatever it is he needs to do for this job he got and Todd will be asleep. Sneak in and peek. If they're there, count how many are missing from the box. That way you could sort of see how heavy the competition is."

"That would never work."

Eileen had always taken any criticism of her elaborate plans in a negative way. She sounded insulted now. "Why not?"

"Because, goofus, say you've got a box of—how many come in a package?"

"I don't know. That's Bob's department."

"Well, okay, say there's twelve in a box."

"Okay, and say three are missing. That would mean—"

"It would mean exactly nothing unless you knew how long the package had been sitting there in the drawer."

"Ooh, I see what you mean."

"Yeah." Rachel thought about the problem—purely as an intellectual exercise. "Are condoms dated?"

"You mean do they have an expiration date, like milk or yogurt?"

"Yeah."

"I don't know, but that would certainly be helpful, wouldn't it? Maybe they do. After all, I would think they'd get brittle and crack after a while, wouldn't they? They'd be no good then."

"Sounds painful from the female point of view. Eileen?"

"Yes?"

"Does it strike you that we are having a very bizarre conversation here?"

"Reminds me of the overnight we had when we all sat around wondering about the size of Peter Wainright's you-know-what and how he'd ever get it sufficiently covered to be safe in this very type of situation. Remember? It was after that boy's swim meet we went to and we saw all the guys for the first time in those tight little racing suits. I had the hots for that guy for weeks after that. Man alive, he really filled out a swimsuit, didn't he?"

"Eileen! I am hanging up before this conversation degenerates even further—as if that's even possible at this point. I have to call Daniel anyway and confirm that tomorrow's still on."

"Oh, yes, right. That's as good an excuse as any other, Rachel. You just tell yourself whatever you have to to justify calling the man. You know you're dying to talk to him, admit it. You just want to hear his voice again. Just be careful so you don't drool all over the phone. You might short it out and electrocute yourself.''

"Eileen, you're being ridiculous. I haven't heard you sound so adolescent since—well, since we were adolescents. I really mean it. I'm hanging up. Goodbye.''

"Bye. Call me tomorrow night.''

"Maybe. I'm beginning to think we share entirely too much.''

"Ooh, this *is* serious then.''

"Oh, shut up.'' And Rachel hung up on her sister for the first time in a long time.

The phone was still warm, however, when she had Daniel's number from directory assistance and was punching in the digits. She gripped the receiver tightly as Daniel answered.

"Hello?''

"Daniel? It's me, Rachel. I was calling to confirm about tomorrow. Are we still on?'' Gee, it sounded important when she put it like that. Like a real date or something. Too bad it was nothing more than a baby-sitting job.

Rachel told herself to stop worrying, that everything would be okay. At some point before she died, probably when she was around eighty years old, Rachel just knew she'd find somebody who would appreciate her simply for herself. Someday, her prince would come. If she didn't believe that, she'd probably kill herself. Let's just hope she wasn't too senile to appreciate the man when he finally showed up on her doorstep.

"You can still come, can't you?''

Daniel sounded a bit panicked, which pleased Rachel. Somebody needed her. For her way with children, if for no other reason. She was needed.

"Yes, I can still come. I wanted to make sure you still needed me, that's all."

"Yes. Yes, I do. In fact, I wish there were two of you, if you want to know the truth."

He sounded weird. "Daniel?"

"Yes?"

"Is everything okay? You sound, I don't know, hassled, on edge."

"That's because I am," he said and she could almost hear his hand raking through his hair. "Don't get me wrong, I'm delighted to have the phone ringing, believe you me. It's just that I'm already swamped, which is a good problem to have, I know. Certainly better than the opposite. But I would really love to have you along helping me count cars. Unfortunately you're also the only one I trust with Todd."

Rachel glowed and hugged the knowledge that he wanted her with him. "No one's answered your ad yet?"

"Nobody I've had time to check out and it's not like I can put this off to another time. The car dealership's made arrangements to close down for the day tomorrow so I can inventory the lot. Ready or not, I go. That's all there is to it. I'll probably be out there forever trying to finish up in one day."

"But the temperature's supposed to drop into the low fifties and they've forecast rain for tomorrow!"

"Great. Just great." He sneezed. "Did you hear that? I'm getting sick in anticipation of being miserable out in the cold and wet tomorrow. Oh well, you'll just have to keep a flame going under the teakettle while I'm out, I guess. Like I said, there's no getting out of it, not if I want to start building up my firm's reputation." He sneezed again. "I just wish there was some way to clone either you or me so we could be in two places at once."

Rachel spoke without thinking. "If we found some-one else to stay with Todd, I could come help you. That would work out, wouldn't it?" Why would she put her-self through another day of torture being near a man burnt out on love—the one thing she craved? Obvi-ously, she was in a sorry, sorry state.

Daniel interrupted her self-castigation. "Rachel, you're the only one I trust with Todd. The college girls I've interviewed so far just don't have your maturity."

Rachel didn't know if she was insulted or not. "I'll call my sister, Eileen. She'd be terrific with Todd. And she's two years more mature than even I am. It'll be perfect, you'll see." Rachel chewed her thumbnail while she thought. Hmm, it was a good plan. Eileen's daugh-ter was in high school and gone all day. Eileen would enjoy being around a little one again. And Eileen could check the nightstand drawer for Rachel while she was there. What a brilliant idea.

"Rachel, I appreciate the thought, really I do, but I don't know about this—"

"It'll work, you'll see. In fact, I'm going to hang up and call her right now. I'll see you in the morning. This'll be fun. I can hardly wait."

"Wait, Rachel, I—" But Daniel was speaking to the dial tone. He hung up feeling slightly dazed by the en-counter. Rachel had taken charge—with a vengeance. He left his study, going out to the kitchen to fill the coffee-maker. He needed a jolt of caffeine. Maybe it would clear his head and he'd be better able to figure out what had just happened.

Rachel was at his door at eight o'clock on the dot the next morning with a slightly distorted carbon copy of herself in tow. "Hi," she greeted him. "This is my sister, Eileen. Are you ready to go?"

Rachel looked professional, but warm in black tailored slacks and a gray cashmere sweater under a shiny white rain slicker. Daniel would quite happily count cars or anything else Rachel cared to count as long as she was by his side. Body parts could be good, he thought. Rachel had a few he wouldn't mind inventorying.

Daniel sighed and raked a hand through his hair, hoping his strong attraction for Rachel wouldn't make itself evident at that moment. His body's reactions around Rachel could be embarrassing. Turning to her sister, he said, "Nice to meet you, Eileen. I appreciate your coming on such short notice. Please come in. I'll introduce you to Todd and show you where things are before we go. I'm sure your sister won't mind waiting that long before we get under way."

Eileen smiled and took the proffered hand, shaking it briefly. "Don't count on it. It's her first real job, even though it's only temporary. She's really looking forward to it."

"Don't talk about me like I'm not here," Rachel instructed. "I'm a little excited, so shoot me."

Daniel could think of other things he'd rather do to her.

"Come on, Eileen," Rachel instructed impatiently. "Let's get with the program. I can hear Todd out in the kitchen. You're going to love him. He's darling."

Daniel rolled his eyes and ushered Eileen in before closing the door and leading them through the living room and down the short back hallway to the kitchen.

"I guess we've got our orders, Eileen. We better move, if we know what's good for us."

Eileen and Rachel had to rush to keep up with Daniel as he paced down the hall, a man now on a mission. Eileen glanced sideways at Rachel and rolled her eyes meaningfully then jerked her head in the direction of Daniel's back. Rachel didn't have to guess too hard to know that Eileen approved of the way his crisply pressed white business shirt stretched carefully over his broad shoulders before tapering down into his navy slacks.

Eileen kissed her fingertips behind his back and mouthed the words *muy macho* to Rachel who made frantic shushing motions as they moved as a group down the hall.

"Eileen, this is my main man, Todd. Todd, don't eat that off the floor. It's dirty now." Daniel moved around the kitchen, showing Eileen the various points of interest. "This is his favorite cup. Here's where I keep the bibs. There are hot dogs in the refrigerator for lunch, but you have to cut them longitudinally before you slice them, otherwise he might choke. Canned peaches and peas are up in that cabinet and if he doesn't eat right at noon and then go down for a nap, he gets cranky."

"Todd, put your hands behind your back and come give me a kiss goodbye. Don't touch my pants, whatever you do," Daniel warned. Todd moved toward him and Daniel leaned down, carefully trapping his tie against his shirt with one hand so it wouldn't accidentally brush into the yogurt smeared across Todd's cheek. Daniel kissed his nephew on the top of his little head before straightening back up, picking up the raincoat resting over a kitchen chair back and taking Rachel's arm to usher her to the back door. "The car's in the garage," he explained. "Thanks for doing this, Eileen. His diapers are stacked in a hanging thing on his closet door, right through there, and he won't fall asleep without the blanket with the satin binding. Todd, you be good for Auntie Eileen. I'll be back before you know it. We'll have macaroni for dinner, okay, champ? You'll like that. Bye. See you in a while, kid."

Rachel practically pulled him out the door. "Come on, Daniel, we're going to be late."

"Yes, but—"

"He's going to be fine. Eileen is terrific with little kids. She was already washing him up when we left. You didn't hear him objecting, did you?"

"No, but—"

"Stop worrying, she's an old hand, I tell you."

They were halfway down the sidewalk that bisected the backyard and led to the garage sitting on the far rear of the lot. Daniel stopped cold and Rachel couldn't budge him. "Now what?"

"I'll be right back. I forgot to show her where the emergency numbers are posted."

"She knows how to call 911."

"She doesn't know where we'll be, though, in case something important comes up and she needs to reach us," Daniel insisted stubbornly.

Rachel didn't like it, but had to admit he was right. She especially didn't like that he'd thought of it and she hadn't. "You taped it up by the phone I imagine?"

"Yeah. The kitchen phone, not the one in the study."

"Fine, you go warm the car up. I'll run back and show her." No way was she going to risk Eileen making any more approving motions or comments around Daniel.

After doing that and getting thoroughly wet in the process of running back and forth, her raincoat flapping, they were on their way.

"This is a small dealership," Daniel explained as he navigated the soggy streets. The rain had been accompanied by light fog, which made the snug interior of the car feel all the more intimate as the outside world faded. Valiantly, Daniel tried to ignore the sensation of there being no one else in the universe but Rachel and him. "We'll be counting every car," he explained a bit desperately. "A larger dealership we'd just sample, but then a larger dealership wouldn't be coming to a small firm like mine, either. They'd go to one of the big accounting houses, instead."

Rachel listened intently, but all she could really focus on were Daniel's hands, so firm and capable-looking there on the steering wheel. Those were hands you could trust, Rachel decided as she watched them. And while she liked that about him, admired it even, Rachel was forced to admit she was a lot more interested in another function she felt sure those hands could perform—that of ardent lover.

"You're going to have to check the vehicle number of every car on that lot."

She couldn't drag her eyes away from them. What would those hands feel like on her body?

"Make note of the exact date of delivery."

Her breasts swelled just thinking about it.

"There's an incredible amount of loan interest at stake."

Rachel was interested all right. Her nipples had hardened into little nubs and suddenly the pressure of the fabric of her blouse was too much, becoming almost painful to her sensitized breasts. Rachel shifted uncomfortably in her seat, still eyeing those long fingers with great speculation.

"This is it. I hope you knew what you were getting into and aren't disappointed."

Oh, yes. She was ready and she highly doubted she'd be disappointed. Rachel's legs parted slightly, all by themselves.

"Rachel, did you hear me? We're there—here."

What? "Oh. The car dealership." Carefully she brought her legs together and folded her hands primly over her knees. "Sorry, Daniel. I'm afraid I was wool-gathering for a minute there." She closed her eyes briefly in heavenly supplication after Daniel's quick, odd look in her direction. What must he think of her? Thank God he couldn't have any idea what she'd been thinking.

Rachel quickly glanced over again. He couldn't, could he?

Daniel turned to reach for his briefcase and caught Rachel's odd look. "What? Is there something on my face? Did Todd get me with his yogurt after all?"

Rachel shook her head, denying any such possibility. "No, it's nothing. Really."

He watched, fascinated as her hair flew from side to side with the shaking, then settled back into place look-ing slightly tousled now. If he mentioned it, she, being female, would probably shriek and grab for her hair-brush. But the fact was he thought Rachel looked ador-able with her hair a bit mussed and her little body all zipped into that shiny white rain slicker. "Then why were you staring?" he asked.

"Oh. Well, I've never seen you all dressed up before, you know. You look very nice. Um, handsome, even."

"Uh-huh." She was lying, and badly at that. It made him wonder all the more what she'd been thinking about. He grabbed his briefcase and opened his door. "Thank you. You look nice, too."

Rachel opened her own door and climbed out. "Thanks," she said as they met behind the car.

Daniel held her arm and guided her into the dealership. He'd tried to cover the prurient desire Rachel raised
in him by chatting about business. He hadn't inadvertently said something totally politically incorrect, had
he? What if he'd said something really tacky like, we'll
be counting all your breasts today instead of all the ve-
hicles? Surely Rachel would have responded with more
than an odd look.

Wouldn't she?

Oh, man. Now he was going to drive himself crazy
worrying. This was ridiculous. He should never have
agreed to her coming along. If it took until midnight—
and it probably would have, he should have come alone
and counted the damn cars himself. He'd send her home
and—

"Okay, so now what do we do?" Rachel looked
brightly around the offices of the dealership.

Daniel sighed. He'd never get her to leave. This was
one stubborn woman and she seemed to be having some
kind of adventure. Well, let her see how boring the
business world really could be, although truth be told,
for some reason he was actually looking forward to
counting cars in a cold rain today. Daniel was bright
enough to know it had everything to do with Rachel being there with him, but he decided against trying to dis-
sect or identify his emotions too carefully just then. Live
for the moment, that was his motto.

He showed her the inventory the owner had left. "You
remember what we talked about in the car?"

Not really. She'd been a little too focused on the wonder of Daniel's tapered fingers and broad palms to really take in much else. "Uh, maybe you'd better go over
it one more time." Another close look at those hands
had Rachel questioning if her whole breast wouldn't fit

perfectly right into his palm. She doubted he'd even have to spread his fingers to—

Oh, dear, just listen to her. A few months without a man and she was becoming depraved. It was disgusting. It was reprehensible. It was—the nipples on both of her breasts were tingling. Oh, dear.

"We're going to have to go out in this lovely liquid sunshine and check off every vehicle identification number on this list, then count all the cars to make sure there aren't any on the lot that aren't listed here."

Rachel clicked her heels together and saluted. "Right. Gotcha." She picked up the inventory list and made a production of studying it. "This ridiculously long number here? Do they really make that many cars that they need to use such a big identification number or are they trying to make themselves look big and important?"

"Rachel, maybe we ought to—"

She turned slightly, preventing him from getting a hand back on the inventory list. "No, no, I can do this. I assume this is like, tattooed on the car someplace. Just tell me where."

"It's usually on the dashboard on the driver's side up close to the windshield, but you can also simply find it on the sales sticker on the side window. You should compare a few of those, too, by the way to make sure the right sticker's on the correct car."

Rachel looked from the list to the cars glistening in the rain outside the building's plate-glass window. "Okay. Piece of cake. You take half, I'll take half and let's do it." She pulled the hood of her rain jacket up over her head and headed out the door, clipboard in hand.

"Little does she know this is going to take her most of the day," Daniel muttered as the blinding flash of white headed toward the first row of cars. Daniel plunked a

wide-brimmed waterproofed fedora-type hat on his head
and followed her out.

An hour later, he was frozen through, his hands so
stiff he could hardly hold his pen. Daniel blew his nose,
then waved his arm to attract Rachel's attention, mo-
tioning in the direction of the enclosed showroom.

Rachel came in, pushing her hood off and unzipping
her raincoat as she came through the door. "God, it's
miserable out there."

"You can say that again," Daniel said as he slapped
his hat against his pants leg. Water droplets flew. Daniel tossed the sodden cap on a desktop and headed
straight for the coffeemaker he'd fired up before they'd
gone out. "You must be frozen," he commiserated as he
handed her a foam cup. "This will warm you up."

Rachel wrapped her stiff fingers around the warm
foam and smiled up at him. "Coffee. Thanks for thinking of it, Daniel, that was very thoughtful." And it was.
Her fingers were already warming up. She lifted the cup
and held it against her cheek for a moment. "But to tell
you the truth, ever since I was pregnant with Mark, I
can't stomach the stuff. I don't suppose there's any tea
around anyplace, is there?"

"I don't think so, but there's a machine out in the
customer waiting area that has hot chocolate, I think."

Rachel handed him back the cup. "Thanks. I'll try out
there. Hand me my purse, will you?"

But Daniel pushed her into an orange vinyl chair.
"You sit." He pushed a yellow vinyl chair in front of
her. "Here, take those boots off and put your feet up.
I'll get it."

She felt positively pampered. They went back out
twenty minutes later and worked until noon, only this

time they stayed together. Daniel called out the VINs and
Rachel checked them off the sheet. They laughed and
wisecracked as they made their way around the lot and
Daniel did his best to subtly act as a wind block while
they worked. Rachel needed protecting, even if it was
from her own indomitable spirit and he would make sure
she got it.

For lunch, Rachel found Daniel had preordered in
meatball sandwiches dripping with tomato sauce.
Somehow, he'd gotten them to deliver it with a tea bag
instead of pop. The tea warmed her insides, the meatballs her spirit, but sitting across from Daniel warmed
her soul. The day couldn't be more miserable what with
a constant wind blowing cold and wet down their necks
despite their best efforts to prevent it. Her hands were
numb, her feet blocks of ice and if her nose was half as
red as Daniel's, she looked a sight. Somehow rain had
worked its way in under her hood and Rachel could feel
her hair hanging limply around her face. In spite of it all,
Rachel was having the time of her life. She looked over
at Daniel blowing his nose, then warming his hands over
his meatballs and laughed. This was terrific, the most
fun she'd had in a long time and it all boiled down to
being together, working as a team with Daniel.

Daniel saved the tea bag and managed to make a second cup for Rachel during the afternoon break and
when five o'clock rolled around, he felt like celebrat-
ing.

"It's the end of my first real day on the job," he told
her. "Let's go home and change into dry clothes and go
out to celebrate. How about dinner? My treat."

Rachel had no desire to see their time together end and
wanted to, she really did, but it wasn't wise. "Eileen
needs to get home," she told him. "Her husband, Bob,

and her daughter, Carrie, will be waiting for their dinner."

Daniel thought a little. "Okay, how about if we stop for a movie at the video place and you come back home with me? I'll make dinner and then after Todd conks out we'll watch the movie."

She shouldn't agree. It would be the height of stupidity. She had no willpower when it came to Daniel and she'd probably jump him before the opening credits finished running. But it was too wonderful an opportunity to pass up. "All right," Rachel agreed and couldn't believe she'd said any such thing.

Chapter Nine

At five o'clock, Daniel bundled Rachel into the passenger seat of his car, then popped his trunk open. From there, he retrieved a white-and-red woolen blanket emblazoned with a two-foot-high Indiana University symbol in its center. Sliding in on the driver's side, Daniel reached over and tucked the blanket around Rachel's knees. He steadfastly ignored the extra beat his heart threw in when his arm brushed her breast, and started the engine, turning the heat on full blast. "There. You were an unbelievable trooper today, Rachel." And she had been. There was no way she'd been anything but miserable, but Rachel hadn't complained, not even once. She'd acted as though standing hunched against a freezing wind while cold water hit you in the face and dribbled down your back was nothing but a minor inconvenience. "Just hang in there for another minute or two and I'll have you warmed up in no time."

Fortunately the rain had stopped around three, but it had still been damp and chilly out on the car lot. Rachel snuggled beneath the blanket, luxuriating in its warmth. "I didn't know you graduated from Indiana," she said. "That's where Mark is now, down in Bloomington."

"That's good," Daniel grunted as he backed his car out of its spot. "Friends don't let friends go to Purdue, and all of that," Daniel said, naming the other large state of Indiana university.

"My father graduated from Purdue."

"Oh, I'm sorry. That's too bad." He made it sound as if she'd just announced an incurable disease.

Rachel rolled her eyes. "It's ridiculous for grown men years out of school to still be carrying on that interstate school rivalry. You've been out, what, ten years? And my dad far longer than that. But in my parents' guest bathroom? He has a sign right over the toilet paper holder that says IU diploma and an arrow pointing down. It's ridiculous. He practically stopped speaking to Mark when he decided to go down to Bloomington instead of West Lafayette." She snuggled down inside the blanket and smiled to herself over Daniel's thoughtfulness.

Daniel made a left out of the lot and smiled as the car dealership receded in his rearview mirror. He was determined to watch the traffic rather than Rachel. He did not have any extra cash just then to waste on car repairs if he smashed it up through lack of attention. "Mark made a wise decision. Just wait. Indiana will win back the old oaken bucket trophy this year."

"You mean that football game they play every year where Indiana and Purdue try to kill each other? No way. At least not according to my father."

Daniel smiled evilly and sneezed as he braked for a red light. "Wait. You'll see."

Rachel pulled a clean tissue out of her purse and handed it to him. He even blew his nose with class. "I could understand it better if there was at least a decent-looking trophy at stake, but who would want an old wooden pail anyway?"

"Anybody who's ever gone to IU or Purdue."

"I can see I'm going to have to keep my father and Mark separated this Thanksgiving. One of them will be flying extremely high and unable to resist teasing the other who will be in the depths of despair."

"Probably," Daniel agreed and pulled into a spot in front of a supermarket. Talking about football had kept his mind off sex with Rachel and gotten him this far without crashing. There was only a short distance left to go. "What do you want for dinner? I promised Todd macaroni, but I'll make it tomorrow instead. He'll understand and I want to make you something kind of special for all the hard work you did today. Is there any movie you've especially wanted to see? I can rent one right here, now that I think about it. Eileen might be getting antsy, so if I get the film here, it will save another whole stop."

Rachel looked at Daniel's face and was able to easily read between the lines. He wasn't worried about Eileen, he wanted to get back to Todd. After the past few weeks of having Todd as a constant companion, Daniel missed the little pill-face. Wasn't that the sweetest thing? A smile bloomed on Rachel's face. She started to tug the blanket off. "I'll come in with you."

He tucked the blanket right back up under her chin. "No. You stay here and keep defrosting. I'll take care of this. You've earned it after everything you did for me today. Sit tight. I'll be out in under ten minutes.''

It was closer to twenty, but Rachel got such a head rush when such a handsome-looking guy came out the automatic doors, searched her out where she waited in the car and then smiled at her, *at her,* that the extra ten minutes hardly mattered at all.

Daniel appeared extremely pleased with himself as he stowed the grocery bag in the rear seat and slid behind the wheel.

''What'd you get?''

''Never you just mind. It's a surprise.''

Rachel would have quizzed him further, but he seemed so smug with his secrets that she didn't have the heart and resigned herself to something along the line of a steroidal male movie probably starring Sylvester Stallone and hot dogs. Probably a better grade pork than the other day's, but a hot dog was a hot dog, just as Sylvester, no matter how the moviemaker had decided to show off his biceps, was still Sylvester. Oh well, if Daniel made it for her, she'd eat it. And she'd watch the action flick as well. She just hoped there wasn't *too* much blood and gore. Her stomach would be queasy enough after the hot dog.

Hmm. On the other hand, she could shudder during the especially violent moments. Wouldn't he feel compelled to wrap his arms around her and hold her tight after that?

Rachel started as Daniel pulled back out onto the street.

''What's wrong?'' he asked without taking his eyes off the traffic.

''Nothing. Just a sudden chill down my back.'' But there was something wrong. The significance of her last train of thought was hitting her with enough force to take the wind right out of her lungs. *If Daniel made it for her, she'd eat it.* What? *She'd actually willingly sit through a murder-and-mayhem movie?*

Rachel wheezed a bit as she tried to get air into her suddenly oxygen-starved lungs. No matter all the precautions she'd tried to take, Daniel was getting to her more and more. Here was the living proof. Rachel hated hot dogs only slightly less than she hated guy flicks.

He absolutely was getting to her.

Oh, damn.

Daniel shot her a fleeting glance of concern. "Rachel, are you all right or not?"

"Yeah." She waved her hand in a dismissing gesture and concentrated on sucking in air. "Fine. Really. No problems." Oh, man, what was she supposed to do now? How could she have allowed herself to care?

"I knew I should never have allowed you to talk me into this. You're going to get sick and make me feel guilty for letting you go out in the rain, aren't you?" Daniel slapped the steering wheel in self-disgust. He'd tried to take care of her. Obviously he'd failed. "Damn. Well, hold on. We're almost home." And in fact, he turned right then into the alley that led to the garage behind his house. "Come on. Let's get in and send Eileen home."

They did just that.

"You're not coming with me?" Eileen asked as she shrugged into a heavy Irish knit cardigan.

"Uh, no. I'm going to eat dinner with Daniel and Todd before I go. We'd invite you to stay, but I know you have to get home to Bob and Carrie."

"Yeah, right. Whatever. You just be careful," Eileen muttered close to Rachel's ear as she passed her by in the entrance hall. "The box in the drawer hasn't even been opened yet. Untouched. Virginal, so to speak."

Rachel's eyes widened and she followed Eileen out onto the front porch. "You think he planned this all out ahead of time? He bought them—with *me* in mind?" What an amazing idea. One she wasn't sure quite how to take. Rachel was both insulted to think Daniel thought she was easy and flattered to know she was still attractive enough for him to try.

Eileen shrugged. "Who's to say? The dumb things aren't dated after all. He might have bought it months ago—in which case he's probably primed to jump anything remotely female and I feel duty-bound to point out that you're the only game in town tonight—or it could have been purchased only yesterday specifically with you in mind. Any way you look at it I suspect it may be sink or swim time tonight. Now you listen to Auntie Eileen. You've been out of circulation for a while. These days, men expect a lot for the price of a dinner. Be smart. That little Todd's a sweetie. You can always use him as your buffer if you decide you don't want to, you know? Pretend you hear him crying, or something. I'll call you tomorrow."

"Rachel? What are you doing out there? And without a jacket? Are you determined to get pneumonia?"

Rachel looked back into the house. Daniel was steaming at full throttle through the living room, headed for the open front door. "I'll be right in, Daniel," she called, then whispered, "I'll talk to you later."

"Count on it," Eileen huffed before she reluctantly walked away from the porch and down the sidewalk.

Rachel watched her go, then turned back and went into the house. "I was just saying goodbye to Eileen.

She'd forgotten how much fun the little ones are. She said she liked Todd."

"What's not to like?" Daniel grumped as he reached around her to close the door, then rubbed his hands up and down her arms. "He's a cute kid. Just feel your arms. You've gotten yourself chilled all over again."

"Stop fussing, Daniel. I'm fine." The denial lost some of its effectiveness, however, when she sniffled.

Daniel rolled his eyes. "Come on. Dinner's just about ready."

"What can I do to help?" Rachel asked as she followed him out to the kitchen.

"Nothing," he announced proudly. "It's all taken care of. Just wash up and sit down."

The kitchen smelled heavenly, and it sure as all heck wasn't hot dogs. Rachel was suddenly absolutely starved. "Daniel, what have you got cooking? God, it smells good."

Daniel opened the oven door and, hot pad in hand, pulled out a tray of three golden brown breaded chicken breasts. "I got chicken Kiev all premade from the gourmet meat area," he announced as proudly as if he'd come up with the dish himself. "All you have to do is heat them through. Here's good Italian bread from the bakery and real butter. And look, I got this bag from the produce aisle that comes with everything you need— lettuce, croutons, salad dressing, everything for a Caesar salad." He pointed to a bowl on the table. "And there's cut-up fruit from the store's salad bar. Pretty good, huh?"

"It looks great," Rachel said and meant it.

Within five minutes, silence reigned. Dinner was too good to do anything but concentrate on every cholesterol-laden mouthful. Even Todd seemed to sense the difference. Very little of his meal found its way to the floor.

A short while later, Daniel sat back in his chair. He reached for the wine he'd poured and took a sip before sighing contentedly. "I guess I didn't realize how hungry I was. I really enjoyed that."

Rachel's plate was virtually spotless. "It was terrific," she admitted. "I'm stuffed."

"I hope you saved room for dessert. I found an incredible-looking chocolate cake in the bakery area."

"Oh, God." But she couldn't, Rachel decided. At least not right then. Rachel waved her hand. "Sorry. My eyes were definitely bigger than my stomach tonight, I'm afraid."

"We'll save it for the movie," Daniel decided. "I'll stack these dishes in the sink, give Todd his bath and pop him into his crib and we'll start it." He rose to set his outline for the next half an hour into motion.

Rachel got up at the same time. "I'll help with the kitchen or the bath, your choice."

But Daniel was already collecting the dirty plates. "No, no, you've done enough today. I'm actually starting to get good at all this. You might as well go in and put your feet up." Conserve your energy because old Daniel had had a good day and was feeling frisky tonight.

Rachel watched for a minute and began to feel decidedly superfluous. Daniel divided his time between filling the sink with soapy water, in which he put the dishes to soak, carefully wiping Todd's face and hands before setting him free, and cleansing the countertops. He *didn't* need her help. In the short span of time since Rachel had seen them last, Daniel had made a whole ton of progress at growing into the role Fate had thrust on him.

He had metamorphosed into both a father and an up-and-coming businessman.

And what was she? A nothing, that was what—an empty-nested, skill-less—nothing.

"Go pick out three boats, Todd. Can you show me three fingers? One, two, three—good job. Count that many boats. You can bring them into the tub with you."

"'Kay." And Todd took off as fast as his little feet could carry him.

"I'll get him started," Rachel said and rose from her chair.

"You don't have to."

"I want to."

"If you're sure—but make sure he tells you the colors of the boats he brings into the bathroom as he's putting them in the water, okay? He's having a little trouble with blue and green and I want to keep reinforcing those skills."

Rachel had been the one who'd started Daniel counting things and pointing out colors and shapes with Todd! Had he already forgotten that? Of course she'd talk about the colors of the boats! Now she not only felt superfluous, but unappreciated as well. *Humph!*

She went into the bathroom and turned on the tap, then muttered her way through the bathing, diapering and pj-ing process. Putting Todd on her lap, Rachel sat in the bentwood rocker and read him a story. "How many brown bears, Todd? We'll count together. One, two, three. Terrific! Here are their chairs. One, two, three."

And on it went until Todd was tucked into bed with his big blue, square blanket, which became a large blue triangle when folded diagonally in half. "I bet he never thought of that one,'' Rachel muttered as she switched off the light and left the nursery.

She found Daniel in the living room, messing around with all the little buttons behind the hidden panel on the VCR—the ones that regular, normal people didn't touch even if the picture was slightly off for fear of really messing up the reception. "Trouble with the picture?" Rachel asked as she sank onto the sofa.

"It had a slight waver down by the very bottom, but I think I've just about got it—there. Perfect."

Pleased, he turned and smiled at her and once again, Rachel's heart almost flopped out of her chest. Thank the good Lord for rib cages. At least they kept that rather vital organ contained enough to prevent it from falling out onto the floor. God bless her, one of those smiles was going to kill her someday.

Daniel sat next to her on the sofa, kicked off his shoes and put his feet up on the coffee table. That didn't bother her so much. It was the arm he rested along the sofa back and behind her head that kept her heart flopping around like a beached fish behind its retaining wall of bone.

"I didn't make any popcorn. I figured we'd wait a little while for that."

"Good idea."

"Yeah, but I did bring you a glass of pop. It's there on the table beside you."

"Oh, that was nice. Thanks." Rachel took a sip, then set it back down. Then, with nothing left to do with her hands, she sat stiffly and tried to keep from sliding down into the deeper dent Daniel made on the sofa, but it was tough going. She was fighting not only gravity, but her own natural inclinations as well. The previews on the television screen finally faded away and the main feature's music began to swell.

"What's this?" Rachel asked as she leaned forward, suddenly interested. "Cary Grant?"

"And Leslie Caron. *Father Goose*. You ever see it?"

"Once, a long time ago. I'd forgotten about it. As I recall, this is a great movie."

When Rachel settled back into the sofa again, ready to really enjoy herself, Daniel's arm had moved just enough that his hand now brushed her hair. It was incredibly distracting, especially when he started playing with the rain-curled ends, but Rachel decided to be stalwart and not complain.

"It's the perfect date flick. War for the guys, romance for the women. What more can a couple ask?"

Nothing, Rachel thought, becoming engrossed in the film. Cary Grant as an apolitical dropout from life had found himself caught up in World War II and unwillingly marooned on a South Pacific island behind Japanese lines as a plane spotter for the Allies.

Daniel stayed right by her side as circumstances conspired to send Cary across miles and miles of open ocean in a small dinghy to go rescue another spotter from a different island. Too late to save him, Cary finds instead Leslie Caron with a group of young schoolgirls under her charge. Daniel left the room to bring in the cake at that point.

"Is the dumb part over yet?" he asked as he handed her a plate and fork.

"Yes, they're on their way back now. The Japanese destroyer didn't see them, but its wake is about to sink the dinghy."

"All right."

Rachel ate her cake, but she tasted Daniel when Cary finally got around to kissing Leslie.

"He ought to shave before he does that," Daniel said critically. "Women don't like it when you leave them with a bad whisker-burn."

"I doubt she cares," Rachel sighed. "Some men a woman will forgive anything."

"Oh, yeah?" Daniel ran a hand over his cheek and chin. "Well, let's just see about that." He set his plate down, turned to face her, then gently used his hand to turn her head toward him. Gently, he placed his lips over hers. "How about my whiskers? They're not as overgrown as his. What do you think? Do they bother you?" he asked, rubbing his cheek carefully along hers so she could sample their texture.

"Not really." She sighed again and found his lips with hers. It appeared Daniel was one of *those* men.

Japanese warplanes patrolled the skies over Cary's and Leslie's heads, but the twosome was left to cope on their own as Daniel and Rachel lost sight of anything and everything outside of each other. Rachel opened her mouth to him and tasted chocolate. His lips felt cool, but she knew they wouldn't be for long. She ran her tongue along his lips and they warmed quite nicely.

"Daniel?"

"Hmm?"

"Nothing. Just—Daniel."

Daniel leaned back, studying her face with his eyes, learning it with his fingers. He traced her eyebrows, the length of her nose, her full lips.

Rachel sucked his finger into her mouth, lightly nibbling.

In terms of sensual stimulants, it probably wouldn't pull a very high rating, but Daniel was obviously an easy touch. He went wild.

Popping his finger out of her mouth, he took her hand into his. After kissing her palm, Daniel managed to give each one of her fingertips the same sensual bath Rachel had given the one of his.

"Oh my," she murmured as he started on the last one. "My goodness."

"Yeah," he said, in total agreement. "You can say that again."

"Oh my."

Daniel chuckled against her mouth and Rachel gave up the battle, thrilled with the signs of humor he showed. When her body relaxed, Rachel slid down into the deeper depression Daniel's body's bulk caused in the sofa cushion. She ended snuggled right up against him.

"Hello," he said, grinning down.

"Hello, yourself."

"Wanna wrassle around a little bit?"

Rachel ran her hand down his arm. "Well, I don't know."

"The shy kind, huh? Here, I'll help you make up your mind." He kissed her. It was not a straightforward meeting of the lips. No, this kiss was the kind that snuck up on you when you weren't looking and ended up knocking you senseless. Rachel's eyes dilated halfway, as a matter of fact, and by the time Daniel raised his lips, she had to concentrate just to get her eyes to focus.

"That help?" Daniel asked, all consideration and concern.

Rachel gazed up at him in bewilderment. Help? Had he lost his mind? No, it hadn't helped. He'd totally befuddled her mind. They'd been teasing and laughing one minute and the next, well, she'd be lucky if she could remember how to walk after that last kiss. And now, now he was kissing her eyes closed, which was probably good because behind her lids, Rachel was fairly certain her eyes were crossed. For a woman of her advanced years, this was embarrassing.

Her arms. How had they gotten around his neck? Rachel sighed into Daniel's mouth as it returned to hers. Who cared how they'd gotten wrapped around him? They were there. Too late to worry now.

"God, you are so beautiful, Rachel." Daniel leaned back as far as Rachel's arms would allow and studied her. She'd gone soft and limp on him and her eyes had a kind of dazed, unfocused look to them. The woman could make him crazy when she looked frazzled and wore sprinklings of Todd's lunch. But here tonight, curled up in his arms, well, she about knocked him out cold. Daniel ran his hand down Rachel's side, grazing the side of her breast.

She squirmed against him and he was emboldened to explore further. Finesse went out the window and he went for a straightforward capturing of her breast in his palm, then warmed it in his hand. Rachel jerked slightly and Daniel heard a slight hitch in her breath. He smiled.

She was not immune.

Thank God. He'd hate to have to suffer through this madness all by himself. Daniel felt her nipple peaking. It prodded his hand and he wanted nothing more than to pull off her sweater and explore.

Calm down, he ordered himself. *You are not Tarzan, she is not Jane. Take a deep breath.* He made it two, then slid his trembling hands beneath her sweater. Daniel let his mouth molest her creamy throat as his fingers grazed the underside of her breasts. His kisses traveled lower. In the blink of an eye, he was into dangerous territory.

Rachel's breath caught.

Daniel's breath caught.

The room had gone fuzzy, Rachel realized. Everything was blurry. Except for Daniel. Never Daniel.

"How do you do this to me?" she wondered out loud as the dark head bent over her filled her vision. Rachel was unable to stop her fingers from combing through Daniel's thick, rich hair. Then, when his hands traveled up her back to unfasten her brassiere, and he suckled *there,* Rachel was reduced to simply clutching his head, holding him to her breast. Panting was all she could manage. Normal breathing was out of the question.

"You like that?" Daniel asked, grinning, already knowing the answer. Rachel was an honest woman. Her body could not lie. He briefly nuzzled between her breasts before gently moving to the other nipple.

"Oh my," Rachel all but groaned at the intense sensation he produced. "Daniel, I—"

Suddenly all hell broke loose as Japanese warplanes strafed Cary and Leslie's island hut, interrupting a very romantic marriage ceremony via radio. Daniel jerked at the intrusion.

"Ouch," Rachel said and covered the flesh he'd inadvertently nipped.

"God, I'm sorry," Daniel said, horrified. "Did I hurt you?"

"No, no," Rachel quickly denied the possibility. "It was more the surprise."

They both sank against the sofa back. Daniel raked a hand through his hair while Rachel, bleary-eyed, watched Cary wrap a bandage around Leslie's finger in lieu of a wedding ring.

"Get the hell out of there," Daniel advised as he took in the action on the screen for the first time in minutes. This was no time to get mushy. "Those planes will be back." Daniel leaned back and closed his eyes as his advice to Cary echoed around in his brain.

"They got married?" Rachel asked dumbly. "Oh, yeah. I remember that. Sort of."

The final scene, a really great escape with bombs going off everywhere, and an Allied submarine, Japanese destroyer and Cary's little cruiser all joining in the fray was about to start, but Daniel zapped the TV with the remote control. His brain was frazzled enough without the Japanese navy and air force adding to the confusion. He'd never met another woman who could twist him into as many knots as Rachel could. His advice to Cary held for himself as well. This was no time in his life to go getting mushy. He needed all his faculties to be razor sharp, his mind unclouded. He needed to get the hell out of there.

Only there was no place to go. Rachel lived only a couple of houses away. Then it hit him. He'd been fighting the idea of love and marriage with everything he had. *But*, what if you went into it with your eyes opened? What if, like those early all male pioneer settlers out West who wrote ads for wives so they'd have help homesteading, he married for something other than love? He, like them, would have the advantages and attendant conveniences of being married, but without the romance and mush to wade through. There was nothing like love to bring a man to his knees, Daniel knew.

The more Daniel thought about it, the better he liked the idea. It was a good plan. In fact, it was a terrific plan, one of his better flashes of brilliance. Daniel turned to Rachel, eager to share his incredibly insightful idea for getting both their lives back on track with one easy blow to find Rachel wearing a dazed, confused look on her face.

"Is it over?" she asked, still staring at the empty screen.

"All but the shouting," Daniel assured her, pleased to find her still wrapped in a sensual fog. That part of their life together wouldn't suffer. She was an incredible woman and he'd be a fool to let her slip away. And he was not a stupid man.

"Oh." Rachel nodded, although she wasn't focused enough to really understand.

"Rachel—" Daniel shifted positions, trying to find the right one for what he had to say. "Rachel—" He rested one ankle on the opposing knee and dropped his hand down to rest on his thigh. All by itself, the suspended foot began to bob. "Rachel—"

"What? *What?*"

Daniel drew his head back. "No need to get testy."

"You've said *Rachel* three times now, and that wasn't the end of the movie. I remember now. Cary Grant almost gets blown up, in fact, Leslie Caron thinks he was. Then when he finally surfaces, he tips over the dinghy she and the girls were waiting in and dumps everybody into the ocean. There's this really great scene where they kiss and make up at the very end. You turned it off too soon. I wanted to see them kiss again." She touched her own throbbing lips. Heck, she wanted to *be* kissed again. Who wanted it vicariously when Daniel was less than a foot away? She never thought to see the day, but frankly, Leslie could have Cary with her blessings if she could just have Daniel.

"Okay, okay," he soothed. "I'll start the tape back up in a minute. Just let me say this one thing, all right? Oh, man, is that Todd I hear? He couldn't be waking up, could he?''

Wasn't that her line? Reality was coming back in a rush. She was the one who was supposed to use Todd as an excuse to break things up. Rachel listened as she struggled to refasten her bra beneath her sweater. He really was awake. And crying. "Maybe he had a nightmare. Monsters under the bed or something."

Daniel stood up. "Great. That's just terrific. I've got to go in to him." He angled his body toward the hall, then back toward Rachel. Daniel began backing out of the room, talking extremely rapidly all the while. He had to say it before he lost his nerve—or Rachel. "Listen, Rachel, this is not how I wanted this to happen, but I just want to say I've been thinking about both of our situations, and—oh shoot, he's really wailing now." Daniel talked even faster. "I just think you can fill a lot of the needs I have in my life right now and I can do the same for you.''

Daniel was practically out of the room now. "I need office help, you want a job. I need help with Todd, you're terrific with kids. See what I mean?" he asked "So, I'm asking you to marry me." He grimaced. "I know this is not very romantic. But both of us are—" he picked his words carefully "—old enough, no *mature* enough, I think to not need the red hearts and flowers, aren't we? I mean, we'd go into this thing with our eyes open, which would eliminate any possibility of getting hurt, don't you think? If you're not wearing rose-colored glasses, you never have to take them off, do you? Oh, God, this is not how I wanted to do this. Listen, I've got to go to him, but just think about it, all right? Just think about it. I'll be right back, okay?" And with that bomb—one worthy of the Japanese air force now that she thought about it, he was gone.

Rachel sat on the sofa, her knees primly together, her hands on top of them and stared after him. In fact, she sat there for several moments, dazed, before shaking her head, rising and letting herself out the front door. It was an indication of her mental state that she didn't even think to carry their plates out to the kitchen sink. Daniel would find them still sitting on the sofa's end tables when he got back.

Rachel walked the few houses to her own, let herself in and sat in her own darkened living room for quite a while, just thinking about life and all its vagaries and little oddities.

Chapter Ten

"Hello?"

"Rachel? It's me, Daniel."

"Oh. Hi. How are you?"

"Uh, fine. I wanted to apologize for tonight. By the time I got Todd back down and got back to the living room, you'd already left." And he'd stood there staring at the empty sofa feeling like an idiot. His proposal had been an embarrassment. A presentation like that in the business world would have gotten him fired and he didn't know how to go about correcting things. It shouldn't matter, this being nothing more than an arrangement for their mutual convenience, but it did. God, it did. "I didn't want to leave things like that so I was just calling to—check up on you, I guess. Make sure everything was, I don't know, okay. It was kind of an odd end to the evening, uh, actually sort of an odd end to an odd day as a matter of fact."

Rachel sat in her dark living room, feeling buffeted and dazed. She nodded agreeably there in the dark. "Uh-huh."

"So." Daniel stopped and cleared his throat. "How are you?"

Rachel wound the telephone cord around her wrist, frowned down at her hand and reversed her handiwork. "Fine. Just—fine."

Daniel inhaled cautiously. "Well, that's—good. I'm glad. Rachel?"

"Hmm?"

She heard him take in another big breath and mentally braced.

"I meant it, you know."

Again, Rachel found herself nodding in the dark. Daniel would succeed with his new business. Rachel had no doubts. He was incredibly tenacious, unbelievably goal oriented and totally determined. "Did you?"

"I usually have more finesse, you know, but my life has been a little hard to keep running smoothly lately."

Rachel's nod was on the verge of becoming a permanent tick, but she had to agree with his analysis of the situation. His life had taken an unforeseeable and bizarre twist and he wanted her to come in and organize it, as she had her linen closet. "Uh-huh."

A few houses down, Daniel sighed. The sound carried perfectly. "What I'm trying to say here is that I wasn't carried away with the moment or anything, Rachel. The proposal was genuine and I'm asking you to seriously consider it."

"Daniel?"

"What?"

"I don't suppose you—love me, or anything like that, do you?"

He sighed, more gustily. "In all honesty, love's not a subject I'm real comfortable with, Rachel. I mean, the one time I thought I was, everything blew up in my face. And in my current situation, realism has to take precedence, you know what I mean? I've got to list the pros and cons, make rational choices. There's no room in my life anymore for mistakes of any kind. Now logically speaking, after a great deal of thought, this should work for the two of us. Our needs and personality types complement each other fairly well, I think."

Rachel's head continued to keep time with some unheard symphony, although she was no longer sure she was in total agreement with Daniel. "Yes, well, I was just wondering. Love would be a nice addition to your little equation, I would think. But I'll—think about it, weigh my own pros and cons and get back to you, all right?"

What could he say? "Sure, Rachel, sure. No problem. Uh, how long do you think that will take?"

"Do you mean should you go ahead and hire that part-time girl from St. Mary's?"

"Well, yeah, I guess."

"Maybe you'd better. I really couldn't say for sure right now how long I'll need to think on this. I really couldn't."

"Sleep on it," he urged.

She agreed to that. "Yes."

"You'll get back to me?"

"Yes. Sometime soon." Maybe. Provided her brain waves stopped jamming each other's signals.

"Good night, Rachel. Sleep tight."

"Don't let the bed bugs bite," she returned automatically, then blushed at having said something so sophomoric. Rather than apologize—for what, being herself?—she broke the connection, then continued to sit on her sofa in the dark, an odd combination of confusion and depression fighting for mood supremacy. After the experience of her first marriage, Rachel craved being loved to the point it had become an almost physical ache. She wanted Daniel to propose because he was so overwhelmed by her charms that he wanted to put her on a pedestal and adore her, not because she'd be handy to have around on laundry day. She was tired of being nothing more than a convenience. So very tired. The phone rang once more.

"Hello?"

"Hi, Mom."

"Mark!" Nothing like a late night phone call from your only progeny to snap you back to reality. "What are you doing up so late? Don't you have an eight-thirty class in the morning?"

"Mommm—"

Rachel cringed. Less than a minute into the conversation and she'd already blown it.

"I'm old enough to decide my own bedtime, Mom."

"Yes, of course you are. Sorry, I don't know what got into me."

"It's okay," Mark allowed grudgingly. "You probably can't help it." Then he twisted the knife. "I'm pulling an all-nighter. I've got a calculus exam in the morning and a ten-page psych paper due in the afternoon. I'm going to get together with a bunch of other guys in just a little while. We're all going to study together for the rest of the night."

Rachel was quite aware she'd never gone to college and therefore knew nothing about techniques for collegiate success. However, it just seemed to her that no matter how much information you crammed into your brain at three or four in the morning, if you'd been up all night, you'd be so fatigued it would be difficult to draw on that knowledge come test time. She knew better than to say so. "That's nice," she managed to say. "Good luck." Then she bit her tongue before anything else got past her teeth. Rachel desperately wanted to ask about the low-moraled roommate who slept with his girlfriend in the top bunk while Mark tried to sleep down below, but it was a tough subject to bring up tactfully. If she told him to request a roommate transfer, was it possible he could end up with somebody worse? She just didn't have the answers for Mark's questions anymore. When Mark had been Todd's age, things were much more straightforward. The rules were clearer. *Hold my hand when we cross the street or a car will hit you. Don't touch the stovetop or you'll get burned.* Use a condom or you'll get an STD? It just didn't have the same ring to it.

"Mom?"

"Yes?" she responded, still preoccupied.

"Is there any purpose to any of this?"

That stopped her. "I beg your pardon?"

"I mean, like, what's it all about? What're we doing here? You know, is there any real meaning to life?"

After the day she'd had, Rachel was darned if she knew. "Uh—"

"I mean, in the long run, we're all going to die anyway, so what's the point?"

Rachel rubbed her temple with her free hand and took a stab in the dark. "Mark, are you by any chance having trouble with calculus or that paper you're supposed to be writing for tomorrow?"

"It's not like I'll ever use calculus once I'm out of here." Mark proceeded to expand on his theme. "Heck, it's not like I'm going to use anything I ever learned in high school or college. It's all a lot of crap. Who wants to be a stressed-out hotshot executive anyway? Money can't make you happy. Take you and Dad. You worked your butts off in pursuit of the almighty dollar. For what? You're splitsville. Poor people can't afford to divorce, you know. Think about it. If I fail calculus, it might be the best thing that ever happened to me. Maybe my marriage would last. Yes, I think I'd rather be uneducated, then the opportunity won't exist for me to be seduced by the lure of materialism like your whole entire generation was. Always wanting a bigger house, bigger boat, never satisfied. You know what they say, Mom, life's a sh—"

"Don't say it," his mother warned, not even bothering to point out that she did not know a single person who owned even so much as a rowboat. A bigger house? She looked around her in the dark. Not so's you'd notice. But then Mark was not interested in facts right then, he was up on his soapbox. "Not in front of me."

"Uh, life is a ... refuse sandwich and every day you take another bite. Who needs it?"

Mark's timing was impeccable, as usual. Rachel simply wasn't up to handling a son gone philosophical tonight, not after the spanner Daniel had thrown into her works. She really wasn't in the mood for dealing with his sweeping generalizations, either.

Rachel shut her eyes and leaned back against the cushions. Life was so incredibly complicated at times, but to struggle so hard and have it be meaningless as well? Maybe she ought to just shoot herself. Ron certainly wouldn't miss her. Mark's grief could probably be bought with the small inheritance he'd get. No doubt he could be persuaded to set aside his newfound antimaterialism long enough to pick out a shiny new motorcycle, and Daniel? He'd have the girl from St. Mary's. One look at Daniel and whoever it was would agree to a marriage of convenience, which was basically what he was offering, it seemed to her, in nothing flat. Maybe the girl would be a vegetarian like Mark's new girlfriend, she thought deviously, and drive Daniel crazy. Rachel certainly hoped so.

How small of her.

Opening her eyes once again, Rachel stared out the living-room window at the halo around the street lamp. "Well," she began cautiously, "people have been trying to understand the deeper levels of the human experience for thousands of years, Mark. Probably as long as man has been on the planet, as a matter of fact."

"It just all seems so pointless," her son complained.

God, she hoped not. "Yes, well, Socrates, Plato, all the great thinkers grappled with this very problem. They spent their entire lives stewing over the meaning of life. And, in the long run, I'm not sure that any of them came up with anything terribly conclusive. Quite frankly, Mark, you're probably better off not worrying about the cosmic meaning of calculus. Study for the test, then tackle the paper you've let go too long.

"Do the best you can with each day and then if it turns out that higher mathematics *does* play an important role in the meaning of life, why you'll be ahead of the game, won't you? On the other hand, if there's nothing there after you die, you'll never know, will you, so it won't be a problem.

"What you said about all of us dying in the long run anyway is certainly true, but you still have to get from here to there, don't you, and you've got to fill up the time somehow. What're you going to do? Spend it living in a cardboard box on a street corner swilling cheap wine because you haven't got any job skills?''

And now for the really big guns.

''It's easy to sneer at money now while you're living on parental handouts. Drop out of school and you're on your own, buster. Believe you me, you won't have the time to worry about cosmic significance then. You'll be too tired from working three jobs just to put food on the table to worry about much of anything but falling into bed,'' Rachel warned then found herself wondering if Mark had gotten the ten dollars she'd sent him and if he needed any more. She just managed not to ask.

Dead silence met her little homily. Then he asked, ''You wouldn't support me if I drop out?''

''No.''

''That's pretty cheap, don't you think? And your reasoning's a little shallow, too, in my opinion.''

So she'd disappointed him and would have to add cheap and shallow to her long list of flaws. What else was new? ''Maybe,'' she agreed. ''But it's also real and I'm afraid I haven't got anything more erudite or perceptive that I can say on the subject. I didn't get to go to college and I'll personally murder you if you don't take full advantage of this opportunity for me.''

Mark sighed into her ear. ''Ah, the mother guilt trip. Now *that* I understand. Listen, I gotta go meet the guys. It's eleven-thirty.''

''Okay. Study hard and next time don't leave it for the last minute. It's been a slice, Mark.''

Her son snorted. ''You are so out of it,'' he said and hung up. Rachel stayed where she was for quite a while. It was well after midnight and she still hadn't figured out herself, her son, her future, or the meaning of life when she finally roused enough to climb into bed.

Her sister, Eileen, rang the doorbell bright and early the next morning. "Hi," she said when Rachel opened the door.

"Hi, yourself. It's not even eight o'clock in the morning. What are you doing here?"

"I told you I'd want to hear all the gory details."

"So you did." Rachel sighed. "You could have waited until a decent hour, though," she said, shutting the door after Eileen and trailing her through the apartment to the kitchen.

"Carrie missed her bus," Eileen reported over her shoulder. "So I had to drive her. I was on empty, so I stopped to fill up the tank and ended up buying doughnuts at the gas station." She shook the little white bag in her hand at that point. "And you're usually up at the crack of dawn anyway. Look at you, still in your robe and your hair full of bird's nests. Must have been a big night after all. Come tell me all about it."

Rachel sighed and moved over to the rangetop. Let your life get a little out of hand and before you knew it, it had snowballed completely out of control. "I'll put on the kettle."

"Got a plate and a knife?" Eileen inquired. "I'll cut up the doughnuts so we can share. I got four different kinds."

Rachel handed Eileen the requested items, then sat heavily in the chair opposite her.

"You look completely washed out and exhausted," Eileen commented. "Good night?"

Rachel studied her sister through slitted lids. "Eileen, do you know the meaning of life?"

"Good grief. No. Does anybody?"

"Am I a shallow person because I don't brood over my lack of understanding?"

"Oh, for crying out loud."

The teakettle began to whistle and Rachel rose to fill their mugs. "I'm serious," she said as she plopped tea bags in after the water, then bobbed them up and down as the water began to tint.

"I'm serious," Eileen mocked, as she tapped the knife on the edge of the doughnut plate. Finally she sat back and folded her arms over her chest as Rachel returned to the table and set a steaming mug before her. "It was not a good night, then. The box of condoms is still waiting to be christened. Too bad. Get me a spoon and tell me what happened."

Rachel rose again. "Here."

"Thanks." They both stirred their tea, lifted the bags out with the spoon, wrapped the tea bag's string around the spoon and bag to squeeze out as much liquid as possible, then set the spoon and bag aside. It was a sisterly ritual kind of thing, done almost in unison.

"Come on." Eileen prodded. "So talk, already."

Rachel leaned forward, took a cautious sip, then gasped as she burnt her tongue.

"You always do that," Eileen told her. "When are you going to learn to wait a minute?"

"Probably around the same time I figure out the meaning of life."

Eileen picked up a quarter of a powdered sugar doughnut and bit down. "You'll die first."

Rachel didn't argue the point. It was probably true. She freed her spoon from the tea bag and its string. She lifted a spoonful of liquid out of her mug and let it dribble back in. "Daniel proposed," she announced baldly. "I got totally confused, so I left. He called here. I clarified with him that he doesn't love me but is only interested in a marriage of convenience kind of thing, which is an important point of consideration, I would think. Of course, if there's no meaning to life, maybe not, I don't know anymore." Rachel paused to take a breath.

Eileen was relieved. She took one, too.

"Then Mark called. Maybe I should have Ron get back to him. Do you think Ron knows the meaning of life?"

Eileen burnt her own tongue, she was so taken aback. "That horse's patoot? Are you crazy? He's lucky if he can figure out which side of the bed to roll out of in the morning. I think he took one too many football hits back in high school."

Rachel sighed. "Maybe *I'm* the crazy one."

"You're not as nuts as Ron," Eileen loyally insisted, although Rachel noticed she didn't deny the possibility.

"If that child he's currently dating is a day over eighteen, I'll clean his house for free for a month of Sundays." Eileen rose and retrieved two ice cubes from the freezer. She plopped one in each of their mugs. Silence reigned briefly. "All of that came up last night? No wonder you look a trifle worse for the wear."

Rachel shook her hair back. "I've been under a bit of a strain," she muttered.

"I guess." Eileen picked up her mug, took a drink, then eyed Rachel speculatively. "So what are you going to do? About Daniel, I mean."

Rachel raised an eyebrow. "You don't care about Mark?"

Eileen pooh-poohed her son. "It's just a stage. He'll be fine. Some cute girl will come sashaying on by and hit him broadside. He'll figure out what life's driving force is real quick like and the meaning of life will take on all new significance."

"Oh, great. That certainly relieves my mind."

"No problem. Now about Daniel—there's a guy that might actually need you and there's a lot to be said for being needed, Rach."

"I know, I know," Rachel cried in genuine anguish. "But what about my needs?"

"What are they?" Eileen asked, interested.

"Well, I know this much, the main one is to be loved," Rachel shot back unhesitatingly.

"Yes," Eileen sighed. "I can understand that. I guess I've always taken that much for granted."

"Bob's always loved you, right from the very beginning," Rachel said, sounding for all the world like a petulant two-year-old.

"Well, maybe not *all* the time, but I'll give you most of the time. I love him most of the time, too."

"I know." Rachel banged her cup on the tabletop. "It shows. And besides, Daniel doesn't even really need me, you know. He just thinks he does. Why, you should have seen how much more competent he was around Todd last night. He's every bit as good with that little boy as I could ever be."

"He's still only one person."

"He can hire a girl to come in and be just fine."

Eileen's brow furled. "I suppose so." She sighed. "It's too bad you couldn't just have a fling with him. I've never had one and I can't help but think vicarious thrills would be better than no thrills at all. Then again, you've never been very cooperative. Well, I suppose that leaves you with going out there and getting a job, just like you said before. Did you ever call about that computer class?''

"Yes. It starts next week.''

"That's good, then. It'll keep you busy.'' Eileen stood and removed their mugs. She rinsed them out in the sink, then set them there. "So when are you going to hit Daniel with the bad news?''

Rachel winced. Why did Eileen's words cut so badly? She knew she'd have to inform Daniel of her decision, of course she knew. "I think I'll wait a couple of weeks,'' Rachel heard herself say. "Give him time to find somebody else and realize how well things can work for him with that kind of more straightforward setup. Then maybe I'll go down and see him. My own life will be more together by then, too. I'll be in class, maybe have a job.'' Rachel snapped her fingers. "I know, I'll bring Todd Mark's collection of Matchbox cars. Todd will love playing in the sand with them. I'll just tell Mark that miniature cars have no real value in the cosmic order of things.''

"Ooh, you are upset with Mark, aren't you? If you really want to get his goat, give Todd his box of plastic soldiers. Mark'll really blow his stack at that.''

Rachel considered the suggestion. "Maybe I just will.''

"You do that.'' Eileen leaned over to kiss her sister's forehead. "Listen, sweetie, I've got to run. You take care. You look much better now that you're feeling more feisty. You had me worried when I first came in. I'll talk to you later.''

Rachel watched Eileen fly out the door. She stood there in the quiet apartment, wondering what time the soap operas started. She picked up the remote control and sat down on the sofa.

By five o'clock that night, she'd realized that compared to the daytime talk shows, her life was a model of normality. Rachel found her car keys and took herself out for some fast food. She'd brood over a hamburger and fries. Cholesterol be damned.

A week had gone by. One whole entire week. Daniel didn't know what to think. Rachel hadn't called, he and Todd hadn't bumped into her at the park or the store. It was as if she'd dropped off the face of the earth.

Had she forgotten his proposition? Was she thinking about it at all? As the days went by without a word, Daniel felt the beginnings of anger. It overpowered the fear of rejection.

"What right does she have to treat an honorable proposal like this?" he asked his monitor screen as he sat at his desk. "Women. Pah, they're all the same." Even as he was saying it, Daniel knew it wasn't true. There was nobody like Rachel.

"Mr. Van Scott?"

Daniel swiveled around in his chair. The girl he'd hired to watch Todd a few hours every day stood in the study doorway. "Yes, Meg?"

"I'm going to take Todd down to the park for a while, all right?"

"That's fine, Meg. I'll see you both in a little while then. Have fun." He turned back around. Fun, hah! He'd almost forgotten the meaning of the word. And it was all Rachel's fault. She'd walked off and left him in an empty world of gray. Just how was he supposed to enjoy himself there?

He snorted to himself. He'd enjoyed himself when Rachel had been around. They'd had fun counting cars in the rain, hadn't they, and watching the Cary Grant movie?

He'd kissed her, and make no mistake, she'd kissed him back.

Daniel bolted up out of his chair. Maybe she was sick. She could have caught a cold from being out in the rain and chilled for so long. Maybe she was in bed right that very moment, dehydrated, delirious, not knowing who or where she was. *That* could be why she hadn't contacted him yet.

He dropped back into his seat.

That was the dumbest, most hysterical reaction he'd ever had. "What in the world is wrong with me?" he asked the empty room. Daniel passed his hand over his face, then watched shooting stars go by. Oh, wait, that was his computer's screen saver doing its job. Daniel glared at the asteroids as they shot across his screen. "All right, so she's probably not dehydrated and delirious. She could still be sick, couldn't she? Wouldn't it be the neighborly thing, strike that, the businesslike, professional thing to do—since she'd been working for me when she'd contracted the cold, after all—for me to go check on her?"

Daniel answered himself. "Of course it would." He nodded to himself. "I think I'll go do just that."

When he heard Meg out in the kitchen starting lunch an hour later, he went out to talk to her. Propping himself in the kitchen doorway, he asked, "Meg, is it possible for you to stay for an hour after Todd goes down, or do you have a class this afternoon?"

Meg looked over her shoulder and shot him a nineteen-year-old's version of a sultry look. "You need me to stay?" she asked.

Daniel did his best to ignore the fluttering eyelashes and pursed lips. "I'd like to run out on a brief errand, if it's possible. Could you stay and listen for Todd?"

Meg gave up fluttering and turned back to the peanut butter and jelly sandwich from which she was removing the crust. "Yeah, I guess, but I've got a two o'clock econ class so I've gotta be out of here no later than one-thirty."

"I'll be sure to be back by then." Daniel glanced at his wrist. "It's almost noon already. I think I'll run out now so I have plenty of time." He turned to Todd waiting for lunch in his high chair. "You be good for Meg," he instructed the toddler before kissing his forehead.

Todd banged his tray with his fist in response. "Sammich! Sammich!"

"It's coming, kiddo." Meg laughed. "Hold your pants on."

Daniel left to the sound of more banging. He paced off the few houses that separated Rachel's two-flat from his bungalow, marched up the sidewalk and stopped cold to think about what he was doing and why. "I'm an idiot," he announced to no one in particular and wheeled around to march back home. He went through the yard to the garage and jumped in his car. He was still in the alley behind the garage as he dialed Eileen on his car phone. It was indicative of his tumultuous state of mind that he was willing to pay the high cellular rates first for information to get Eileen's number, then to talk to Eileen.

"Eileen," he said without preamble, "I'm an idiot."

"No duh," Eileen said.

"I hurt your sister," he said.

"Yes," she agreed. "You did."

"But I'm going to try my best to fix things up," he assured her. "The thing is, I need your help." He went on to describe exactly what he required. Eileen agreed to take over Todd's care for the night. For his plan to work, he needed to be with Rachel tonight—alone. By the time he hung up, Daniel was at the supermarket. Carefully reading the back of a stir-fry vegetable package, Daniel picked up the remaining ingredients he would need for an oriental dinner, then he swung through the first-aid area for a box of bandages and stopped by the video department to renew *Father Goose*. His final errand before going home was at the jeweler's.

At five-thirty, Daniel rang Rachel's bell. After an afternoon of planning and preparing, he was an absolute nervous wreck now. "She's probably not even home. I should have called first," he muttered as he waited. But he'd wanted the evening to be a surprise. "She'll probably laugh in my face. That's why she hasn't called yet. She's too busy laughing."

"Who—Daniel!" Rachel opened the door wide to admit her visitor. "What are you—I mean, nice to see you. Is there something wrong down at the house? You're in another bind?"

It was as he suspected. Rachel assumed that he would only contact her if he needed something from her. Tiredly, Daniel rubbed the back of his neck. He'd realized earlier that he'd never given her any reason to believe differently. How could he have when he was just now seeing beyond the superficial himself? "May I come in?" he asked.

Rachel realized she was blocking the doorway. "Oh. Sure. Sorry." She gestured toward the sofa. "Sit down, sit down."

Daniel put his bag down beside the couch and sat.

Rachel positioned herself in the wing chair. She didn't want to accidentally slide into him. He wasn't Cary Grant and she wasn't Leslie Caron, after all. She'd been reminding herself all week that happy endings only happened in movies and fairy tales, although she couldn't deny a funny feeling in the pit of her stomach as she watched him lean forward and clasp his hands around his knees. Hope? God, she couldn't be that naive at her age. What did she expect, a sudden declaration of deep and abiding love and devotion? Not likely.

They both stared at each other.

Daniel finally broke the silence. "I didn't hear from you. I thought maybe you were sick." She was so damn beautiful, he thought to himself. How could he have been so blind?

"Oh, no, I haven't been ill, just—busy," she finished lamely, thinking about the game shows, talk shows and soaps she'd watched over the past week.

Daniel indicated the open newspaper on the coffee table. "I see you've got the want ads out. Anything interesting?"

"Yes. I've circled a few things to call."

Daniel nodded. "That's nice. Start that computer class yet?"

Rachel nodded. "Just the other day. It was interesting. I even understood most of it."

Oh, hell, he was going to have to bite the bullet and say his piece. "That's good. I'm happy for you. Listen, Rachel, about last week. I'm really sorry for the way I proposed. It was an insult and you deserved better."

Rachel flushed. She was totally taken aback. "Well, uh—"

"I'm here to make it up to you," Daniel told her. He gestured to the grocery bag. "I even brought a peace offering. Dinner. I got a sitter and I'm going to cook it for you."

"You are?" Rachel asked faintly. He'd gotten a sitter for the evening? Left Todd with somebody else just so he could be with her? My goodness, he must really be feeling guilty, she thought.

"That's nice of you, Daniel, but it's really not necessary."

"I insist," Daniel said and he meant it. He was getting a little panicky over her lack of response—Rachel wasn't exactly lying in a gelatinous puddle at his feet. He was damned if he was going to leave without seeing this through, though. "Why don't you put some music on and relax while I go out to the kitchen and get started?"

Rachel, looking sort of shell-shocked, didn't disagree, so he went out to the kitchen before she could gather her wits enough to say no.

Twenty minutes later, he had put together a creditable meal. The rice was a little clumpy, but unburned and the stir-fry was actually quite decent, he decided as he popped a soy-soaked pea pod into his mouth. He'd brought Rachel in some wine and insisted that she stay in the living room. After one last furtive glance around the corner to make sure she'd listened, he reached into the bottom of his bag and removed the tape recorder. Turning the volume all the way up, he set it on the counter and carried the food in. He'd given himself twenty minutes of silent tape before all hell broke loose. He hoped it was enough. He was shaking in his boots. God, grant me courage, he implored as he carried two plates piled high with food into the living room.

"Here we go," he announced and set her plate next to his on the coffee table in front of the sofa. It was a clever move if he said so himself. Now she'd have to come sit by him. "You were enjoying yourself that night at my house until I ruined things," he told her when she gave in and moved next to him, a puzzled look on her face. "I kind of decided to go back and do things over. I don't know what plane spotters on a Pacific Island would eat, probably C rations, but there were Japanese in that movie, too and I thought something oriental would be more appetizing than slop out of a can." God, what a romantic he was. Slop out of a can? Man, he better get his act together—fast before he blew this but good.

"It's good," Rachel assured him after her first bite, and it was. Her mind raced furiously as she tried to figure out what in the world was going on. Daniel didn't need her services anymore, not really. This dinner proved it. So why was he here?

They ate silently for a while, Daniel acutely aware of the tape whirring silently through the machine out in the kitchen. *Say something,* he ordered himself. "Rachel, about the other night—"

Her head snapped up. Finally. "Yes? What about it?"

"Well, I know I gave you the impression that all I wanted was a marriage of convenience kind of thing, and to be honest, at the time that's even what I thought. You needed a job, I needed help, I figured it would be enough."

Her lip began to tremble and two tears worked their way free. They rolled down her cheek as she nodded. She scrubbed her cheeks with her hands. "And being needed wasn't enough for me. I need to be wanted just for myself, can't you understand? And now look," Rachel waved at their empty stained plates. "You don't even really need me. You're handling everything just fine on your own. It's hopeless. I'm sorry I didn't call, but I didn't want to tell you *no* even though I know that's what my answer had to be. Can you understand that at all?'' She hiccuped. "Damn, I hate it when I cry."

Daniel watched several more tears trace their way down her face, then he folded her into his arms and rested his chin on the top of her silky head. "It's good you left me alone for a while," he admitted quietly. "Because you're right. This past week made me realize we don't *need* each other, not in that way. I can hire all the Megs I need and you can get a job at any one of those places." He waved at the newspaper riddled with penciled circles. "You can survive quite nicely without me or Todd." He lifted her chin with one hand and gazed into her eyes. "But you know what I do think?"

"What?" Rachel sniffled.

"I think—" But he couldn't complete the thought because suddenly all hell broke loose in the apartment. They were being bombed. Strafed by airplanes. Shells were exploding practically on top of them.

Rachel shrieked and jumped up off the sofa. "Oh my God, what is that? What's happening?"

"It's the Japanese," Daniel informed her as he pulled her down beside him under the coffee table.

"What?" Rachel looked at him wide-eyed.

"The Japanese," he repeated. "I told Cary they'd come back and here they are."

Rachel glanced wildly around from her position under the table. All her furniture was still intact, the glass still whole in the windows, the curtains motionless despite all the turmoil. Rachel began to slither out from under the table. "Daniel, what is going on here? That's a movie or a tape or something, isn't it?"

Daniel grabbed her by the ankle and pulled her back under. "You're supposed to be impressed by all the trouble I've gone through to create an ambience of romance here," he complained.

"Being bombed and scared witless is romantic?" Rachel asked in disbelief. "You are crazy in the head. Nuts. Cuckoo."

"Damn it, Rachel, I am trying to make a point here. Now get back down here and let me do it."

She had no choice. He still had a hold on her leg and his grip was incredibly strong. She settled back down under the table and glared at him. "So what's the point you're trying to make?" Rachel had to yell in order to be heard over the sharp report of the airplane's machine guns.

Daniel swallowed. Hard. "Well, the point is—what I was trying to demonstrate—that is—Rachel, I've come to realize that what I'd offered you was cold and empty. You're a very loving person and you deserve to be loved in return. There's an emptiness inside of me that is always there since you've stayed away. It's made me realize that I do love you, whether I want to or not. It's there and it's real. Don't you feel it, too?"

Truthfully she had to agree. "Yes."

Daniel gave her a quick squeeze. "I knew it. I think I've known it from the moment you came running out of your apartment to save me."

"I wanted to do CPR on you," Rachel admitted while bombs crashed all around.

Daniel laughed in relief. "I'd have loved it. Seriously I think that marriage of convenience stuff was a cover-up until I built up enough personal courage to admit that I'd fallen in love with you. After my experience with Marie I never wanted to be that dumb again. Now I know, falling in love with you was the smartest move

I've ever made. Please marry me, Rachel. I do need you. I need you to love me. So does Todd.''

She just about strangled him, she squeezed her arms so tightly around his neck. ''Yes, Daniel, yes. I love you, too. I've been so miserable here all week knowing I should call you and give you my answer, but unable to do it, knowing you'd be permanently out of my life once I had.''

''Thank God,'' Daniel prayed fervently, briefly closing his eyes. ''Thank God. Honey, I really, really am sorry for being such a jerk, but at least we've got it all straightened out now. Oh, wait. Except for the ring. I've got it in my back pocket, here we go.'' He handed her the bandage container.

Rachel looked at him, puzzled.

''Father Goose,'' he said. ''Remember? He gives her a bandage for a wedding band. You loved that movie. I wanted it to be just like that for you.'' He urged the metal box on her.

Rachel shook her head as she took it. What a nutcase. Only Daniel would think a bandage was more romantic than a diamond. But he was her nutcase and she loved him. Rachel didn't have the heart to disappoint him. Crazy as it was, she was finding this whole episode terribly romantic. She struggled briefly with the lid, then gasped as she got it open. ''Oh, Daniel, you shouldn't have. Not while your business is struggling.''

''Sure I should have.'' He took the can back and shook the contents out into her hand. ''The business can fail if it means losing you. You're the most important thing in my world now, Rachel, and I wanted to make sure you believed it.''

Staring at the multifaceted glinting diamond ring in her palm, Rachel believed it. ''It's beautiful,'' she breathed, tears again sliding down her cheeks as the meaning of the moment truly sank in. "Daniel?"

"Yeah, honey?"

"The bombs. We've got to turn the bombs off. The landlady lives in the downstairs apartment. She'll call the police."

"She's down at my place eating takeout with Eileen and Todd. We're not bothering anybody. I made sure." He slid the ring on her finger. "There you go. I love you, Leslie."

Rachel held up her hand, laughing as she admired her finger. "And I love you, too, Cary."

An airplane made another strafing run out in the kitchen and Rachel knew. Life really could imitate art after all.

*   *   *   *   *

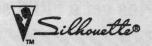

**AVAILABLE THIS
MONTH FROM
SILHOUETTE
ROMANCE®**

#1198 MAD FOR THE DAD
Terry Essig

**#1199 HAVING GABRIEL'S
BABY**
Kristin Morgan

#1200 NEW YEAR'S WIFE
Linda Varner

#1201 FAMILY ADDITION
Rebecca Daniels

#1202 ABOUT THAT KISS
Jayne Addison

**#1203 GROOM ON THE
LOOSE**
Christine Scott

Take 4 bestselling love stories FREE

Plus get a FREE surprise gift!

He's able to change a diaper in three seconds flat.
And melt an unsuspecting heart even more quickly.
But changing his mind about marriage might take some doing!
He's more than a man...
He's a FABULOUS FATHER!

***

January:
MAD FOR THE DAD by Terry Essig (#1198)
Daniel Van Scott asked Rachel Gatlin for advice on raising his nephew—
and soon noticed her charms as both a mother...*and* a woman.

February:
DADDY BY DECISION by Lindsay Longford (#1204)
Rancher Jonas Riley proposed marriage to Jessica McDonald! But
would Jonas still want her when he found out a secret about her
little boy?

March:
MYSTERY MAN by Diana Palmer (#1210)
50th Fabulous Father! Tycoon Canton Rourke was a man of mystery,
but could the beautiful Janine Curtis find his answers with a lifetime
of love?

May:
MY BABY, YOUR SON by Anne Peters (#1222)
Beautiful April Bingham was determined to reclaim her long-lost child.
Could she also rekindle the love of the boy's father?

***

Celebrate fatherhood—and love!—every month.
FABULOUS FATHERS...only in ▼ *Silhouette* ROMANCE™

Bundles of Joy

The biggest romantic surprises come in the smallest packages!

January:

HAVING GABRIEL'S BABY by Kristin Morgan (#1199)

After one night of passion Joelle was expecting! The dad-to-be, rancher Gabriel Lafleur, insisted on marriage. But could they find true love as a family?

April:

YOUR BABY OR MINE? by Marie Ferrarella (#1216)

Single daddy Alec Beckett needed help with his infant daughter! When the lovely Marissa Rogers took the job with an infant of her own, Alec realized he wanted this mom-for-hire *permanently*—as part of a real family!

Don't miss these irresistible Bundles of Joy, coming to you in January and April, only from

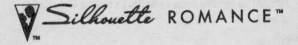

Silhouette ROMANCE™

Look us up on-line at: http://www.romance.net

BOJ-J-A